THE FORBIDDEN LAND

BETTY

The Forbidden Land

LEVIN

namelos
South Hampton, New Hampshire

For Martha Walke

Of all that was done in the past,
you eat the fruit, either rotten or ripe.
—T. S. Eliot

1

Willow peered out from the bed closet. She was rigid, as if poised for flight. Well, what was the point of her waking now if not flight?

She recalled Thorn's unwavering determination to escape. Back then she had felt his desperation without fully understanding it.

Now urgency pulsed in her own legs, in her back, her eyes and ears. Confining stone echoed the muffled sounds of her sleeping father as well as of uncles and their women in adjoining huts. All were close, all sharing this underground dwelling place as they shared fire and food.

Usually their presence brought comfort. But not now. Willow drew her legs up close to her chest, then stretched again. She must stay flexible, ready for action. Now? No, not yet. For if she crept outside now, the dark would hold her captive while she waited for the boys, Crab and Thistle. And maybe for Hazel too? Or maybe not, for Hazel had already begun to submit to the uncles' plan for her.

The uncles wanted new, unflawed infants to take the place of the births that had failed. They would soon pronounce Hazel a woman, and that would put an end to the life she had sometimes shared with Willow and the boys.

Hazel, who had seldom joined in their deeds of skill and their contests of daring, seemed untroubled by what was to come. She had always known that she would be given to an uncle. In time her belly would swell. Then, after a while, there would be a squalling baby. At least that was everyone's fervent hope. Like every mother, she would feed her baby until it could eat chewed food, and then it would be raised by Tall Reed and the other women so that she herself could produce another baby.

But all this could turn out otherwise. Hazel might not fulfill her womanly purpose. That was what Willow's father had said as he looked over the two girls seated side by side. To Willow his appraisal had come like a sharp stab of bitter wind. She and Hazel might just as well have been fish or seals stretched upon the sand, about to be cut into portions.

Willow had understood what it meant. She noticed the eyes of uncles following her while she performed her daily tasks. As they pondered Hazel's frailty, they were already sorting out which of them should father the next child.

Everything—Hazel's lack of vigor, the rarity of new, unflawed children, even the short days that impeded constructing the boat—everything seemed now to bear down upon this cluster of huts like a monstrous wave that threatened to drag them all, Willow included, into the hungry sea. That was why she had pushed Crab and Thistle beyond their limits and even managed to set Hazel at any boat-making task she could perform.

Willow had assured Hazel that this boat would be so great an achievement that all who helped in its making and launching would be remembered in cherished stories. Hazel's poor fingers had bundled and bound reeds until her fingers were raw. Then she had cried out when she dipped them in the sea. Willow had been pitiless, extending her own bloodied palms to show her deeper wounds. Wounds to bear with pride, she proclaimed them.

Probably Hazel was sleeping soundly now, as unconcerned about the boat as she was about becoming a woman and mother. How could anyone be so unquestioning? That was what Willow wondered while she struggled to stay awake for the coming dawn.

Staring out toward the hearth, she failed to see so much as the mound of ashes where she had buried live embers for the morning fire. Not the slightest hint of day filtered down along the underground passageway.

Thorn used to tell her she was too impatient, that she rushed through tasks and ignored exacting details. He would say so now, she supposed. It was true that she had forced and then hurried the making of the boat. And barely in time. At least it would be finished enough to carry her away.

If only she could start now. If only she could prod daylight from the sky.

But in spite of her determination to remain alert, the snuffles and snores of the others finally lulled her. She slept and woke, slept and woke.

When a dim shaft of light finally glanced off the wall, Willow swung around and planted her bare feet on the dried dune grass that covered the stone floor. Quietly she padded into the passage.

The air coming through from outside was still and cold. She considered returning for her heavy sealskin tunic, but she couldn't take the chance of waking someone. Besides, if Crab didn't find her waiting for him, he might retreat. She needed him. She needed both boys to help carry the new boat from the inland marsh and set it in the coastal shallows.

So far they had begrudged the hard pace of the work and questioned every task that had to be undone or tried another way. From the start they had doubted that Willow could recall enough of Thorn's crafting to replicate his basket-like boat. Thistle had even remarked that none of the uncles believed her capable of it either, which was probably why they paid little heed to the boatmaking—as long as Crab and Thistle and Willow performed their regular tasks.

But Willow did pay heed. Every doubt the boys expressed became another goad driving her to succeed. No one would deter her; nothing would be allowed to impede the completion of the boat.

This was the day it would be proven, its bundled reeds tied as firmly as braided grass ropes could be pulled, its feathered wing untested although surely ready for the sea wind. She felt as if her whole life had been a preparation for the launching.

2

To show the boys and to reassure herself that she had attended to every aspect of the crafting, Willow had made a small boat the size of a child's plaything. Now she knelt at the back of the shell heap and dug through sand and rubble where she had hidden it from prying eyes. Let her father and the uncles remain incurious until she was gone from them.

All at once she felt the dog beside her. Thorn's dog. Almost her dog now. He watched as she scooped away debris to uncover the little boat.

But where was Crab, who was charged with waking Thistle at first light? She extracted the small boat and upended it, releasing sand and tiny bones stuck in its grassy network. Inspecting it, she could feel how ready she was, ready for the true boat. She didn't ask herself whether the true boat was ready for her.

This little one hadn't been her first attempt. Two previous small boats had failed to stay afloat in the swamp. After each failure she had berated herself for being too inattentive to Thorn when he had crafted his escape boat. Even though each of her models had resembled Thorn's, only this one had floated boldly and held its shape, bearing the promise of the large craft nearing completion and still shielded among the reeds. This small one, then, had proved a worthy model for the true one that would soon carry her out past the tall rock stack and the treacherous seal ledges, out and out toward the setting sun.

She gazed across the dunes to the flat gray water. There

Thorn had set off on the boat of his making, its wing catching the breeze and providing direction as well as speed, the steering oar holding it on course. She had watched him sail seaward until he vanished from sight.

She dropped her gaze from the empty horizon. Then she cupped the small boat, gently upending it again and letting all the remaining sand sift through its crevices. The dog turned his head aside to avoid the sand, but he kept pace with her as she hastened to the shore.

Pale daylight crept across the dunes. Where was Crab? They should be away from here before the underground sleepers arose. Usually the uncles emerged only briefly. They seemed to feel safer confined in the dark stone huts than in the long, oppressive night that loomed outside. Make haste, she willed Crab. This is our moment.

At the water's edge she drew a breath and then stepped into the shallows. After the first painful shock, her feet and ankles went numb, as if sheathed in ice.

The dog waited on the beach, his eyes fastened on her. Farther out to sea one of the singing seals reared up to watch. Another seal slipped from an outlying rock, a small wave slapping in its wake.

The dog turned, informing her that Crab approached. Stifling a rebuke, she reminded herself that encouragement would set them on firmer ground. Here was a moment to share, a moment rooted in promise. Here the small boat would show itself to be seaworthy.

Leaning down, she let it float from her hands. It wallowed as if uncertain of its purpose. But it was a made thing, not a creature, and of course it lacked its wing. She nudged it gently, then straightened and backed away.

At first it was sucked into the trough she left behind her in the shallows. Then the water became smooth again, and the small boat slid over the surface, bobbing slightly and circling as it floated. She thought of Thorn's boat with its great wing made from diving birds. She had been too pressed to finish the true boat to take more time to craft a tiny wing for this one.

"That is how our true boat will take to the sea," she said to Crab, who stood on the wet sand, a ridge of foam curling around his feet. "Where is Thistle?"

Crab stepped into the shallows, stooped, and fetched a stone from the seabed. Then he splashed after the bobbing craft and dropped the stone onto it. Into it.

The small boat shuddered and wallowed. Then it seemed to shrink and dip as if snagged from below. Water seeped up through its bottom and slowly dribbled in over its sides.

Willow sprang forward to catch it. "That stone was too big!" she charged, rescuing the sodden craft. "You cast it too hard."

Crab said, "The boat we have made is like that. It is not ready for the sea."

"The boat will work," she insisted. "Every day we wait is lost light. I will make the boat work. It must work."

Still standing in the numbing shallows, they faced each other. Then Crab shrugged and splashed back onto the sand. Willow followed. Without Crab she would be nowhere. Speaking to his back, she said, "Hazel is soon to join Uncle Twin Trunk Tree." And it will be my turn next, she felt like adding. Crab didn't seem to realize that she would be under watch, that she would no longer be free to go with him to climb the sea stack or scramble over the headland to the breaking waves.

"Thistle is waiting outside the huts," Crab said. Even if he couldn't understand, he seemed to hear Willow's desperation, just as she had heard Thorn's. "But you should know that Thistle is unwilling to be seen with the boat. He says if it carries you away or if it sinks with you, he and I will be driven into the sea to join you."

"The uncles would never turn on you," Willow retorted. "Because our People dwindle, they need everyone who is young."

"And you?" Crab responded. "They need you, too."

"I must go," she pleaded in a whisper.

"How can you find Thorn on the pathless sea?" Crab asked her.

"I have to try," she answered.

Crab shook his head. "The boat is unready. It is perilous. Tell me why you set forth like this," he demanded.

"To bring Thorn his sun stone," she answered. That had been her stated purpose from the start.

Crab said, "That is not the whole of it. Tell me why you set forth like this *now*."

"I dare not wait," she blurted.

"Not wait for the greening season?"

"I dare not wait," she repeated.

"I think it is the uncles you flee," he said. "You who are the next Keeper of Story."

She couldn't speak. Did Crab really understand her dread of what lay ahead for her if she stayed? Yet he spoke of the greening season to come. He must think she still had time. Probably he trusted the uncles to hold to age-old custom. He could still believe they would make no drastic change as long as the moon waned or the dark of night increased.

"You are needed here," he continued.

"But not for the Story. No longer the Story," she told him. "When the uncles turned against Great Mother, they severed their connection with Story. That is why they flounder now. That is why they fear each coming day. Contrary events surprise and baffle and, yes, torment them. They understand nothing except that the People of the Singing Seals dwindle and are not replenished. So," Willow concluded, "the uncles believe there is only one way for me to serve them."

"No!" Crab protested. "There is more than one way."

He stood with his back to the dawn, the light behind him. She could see no features, only the paleness of his face. She wondered what his eyes would show. For the first time it came to her that he too might long to escape.

She considered what this could mean, to set out with Crab. To be with a companion on whom she had always relied. To enter the unknown world beyond their shore, not alone, but sharing every risk and whatever landfall they came upon. Was this what Crab would choose?

She said, "I may not find Thorn." She faltered. "I cannot know where wave and wind will send the boat." She wanted to say more. She wanted to remind him that Thorn had refused to allow the uncles to possess him. Ever since Thorn's escape and Great Mother's banishment, everything Willow had imagined and attempted had propelled her toward this day. Thorn had shown her not only what was possible but what was necessary. The uncles would not possess her either. She would flee while she could.

She longed to tell Crab that if she remained here she would be lost. But he had already turned on his heel and started back toward the huts. She watched him climb a dune, a tall, straight figure still without defining features because of the low light behind him. She didn't need to see what she knew so well.

All at once she was cold, but not from wading in the shallows. It was a fierce cold that lodged inside her like a thing with shape and substance, as hard as the stone that had flooded her small boat.

Clenching her teeth and shivering violently, she followed Crab's footsteps over the dunes. Too unaccustomed to fear to recognize it, she couldn't imagine how to rid herself of this bitter invasion. She knew only that if she didn't press forward, the cold would overwhelm her and drag her down.

3

Hazel stood outside the huts with Thistle, her shoulders drawn in, her arms clasping her thin body.

Willow couldn't quell her irritation. It erupted in words that could have sounded reassuring but were instead sharp and dismissive. "You might as well stay warm here. The boys and I will bring the boat."

Hazel's teeth chattered as soon as she began to speak. "Not finished," she said.

Willow's thoughts raced back to yesterday, when she had declared the boat finished. Hazel had not spoken then. Crouching to knot a rawhide strip connecting the outer skin to the inner rushes on which she knelt, Hazel had been barely visible inside the craft. As usual, Willow had disregarded her.

Willow supposed that Hazel probably couldn't have spoken then even if she had wanted to. Still, there might have been a squeak of protest from her as she set her teeth and fingers to the task at hand. But Hazel hadn't uttered a word. Even when they were all returning to the huts, even then she could have mentioned unfinished work. She had trailed in silence behind Willow and the boys as they hurried toward the fire and food awaiting them at day's end.

Now when they really needed to make haste, here was Hazel suggesting that she had some task to finish that would surely delay the launching. Thistle placed a protective arm around her bony shoulders. He tried to meet Willow's eyes, but he couldn't face her scorn.

To Willow's surprise, it was Hazel who stood up to her. "There is still work to be done on the boat," Hazel said softly.

Willow shrugged, then started off inland, setting a fast pace for the boys. She didn't look back. Thistle and Crab needed to understand that she was indifferent to Hazel's comings and goings. If they stood by Willow, they would surely agree with her that nothing mattered but getting the boat to the sea before she was prevented from leaving.

Willow didn't slow down until she and the boys approached the crest of the hill overlooking the swamp. Hazel's sharp, tight gasps sounded behind them. Willow swung around to confront the exhausted girl. Why had she come? Surely not to finish tying off a few rawhide fastenings.

Before Willow could think of what to say, Thistle spoke to Hazel. "You did not need to come this far. You can finish the knotting on the beach."

"Yes," Hazel replied, panting. "But I know what to bring and where to find the pieces I made ready. You might have brought the boat without those parts."

Hearing the resolute tone in Hazel's words, Willow was too astonished to comment. She just headed downhill to the boat upended at the edge of the reeds.

Only now, as she and the boys sorted out carry positions, did she realize that they had neglected to attach holding loops. Crab told her he almost remembered how Thorn had made them, but Willow said making them now would take too long. They could wrap their fingers around the bent reeds at the curved edge of the boat's sides. With Thistle, the tallest of them, between the other two carriers, the burden would be shared.

Meanwhile Hazel was gathering up lacings and bundled grasses. "I should finish the outer skin here," she said as the others hoisted up the boat.

The boys turned to glance at her. They knew that if they set the boat down now for her work, another day would be lost.

"Maybe on the beach, then," Hazel told them. "Before you push it into the sea."

Willow nodded absently. Already she was silently reciting to herself the essential things she had made ready in her pouch—Thorn's fire stone, her sealskin boots, dried fish, and a net for catching more. If only she could find a way to wrap a live ember without risk. Well, she would manage anyway.

They had to stop occasionally to change their grip on the boat. Thistle had established the height at which it should be carried, and Willow wouldn't object simply because she was so much shorter. Her shoulders ached from reaching to keep the boat level.

She shifted her thoughts elsewhere. To the wing, which was safely concealed at the back of the shell heap. The wing was smaller than the one on Thorn's boat. But that could be a good thing, she told herself, since she had been unable to find a pole as tall as the great bone from which Thorn's wing had swung. Her smaller wing would still catch and bend to the wind. Her boat would climb each wave and sweep down every trough before swooping upward once more. It would soar aloft on the water.

4

By the time they had staggered over the dunes and set the boat at the water's edge, they were spent. Thistle flopped down on the beach. Crab joined him.

"Since no one is about yet," Willow told them, "I can bring the wing and the pole."

The boys grunted but didn't leap up to help. "It will rain soon," Crab murmured, gazing skyward at the spreading cloud cover.

Willow nodded. Glancing toward the huts, she could see a thin column of smoke rising and hovering above them. "Good," she said. "The uncles dislike rain. They may remain inside a while longer."

She set off toward the shell heap, thinking she might pick up her escape pouch at the same time that she brought the wing to the boat. On her way she caught sight of Hazel trudging over the dunes and dragging some kind of bundle behind her.

As Willow dug out the precious wing, she felt certain she had forgotten nothing. She had even wrapped the wing around its pole for ease of carrying. Still, it made an awkward burden, and she set off with both hands grasping it and no pouch.

Maybe the boys could insert the pole in its prepared socket and secure the wing with the strong grass ropes she'd braided for it. Could they attend to this while she retrieved her pouch? Only if they understood how the wing must be balanced before being fixed in place.

Crab came to meet her on the dunes and hoisted the wing and pole over his shoulder. Once she was able to move her head and neck freely, she looked back anxiously in case any of the uncles had emerged from the huts. She saw no one there, although she did catch another glimpse of Hazel advancing toward the beach. Thistle walked beside her, Hazel's bundle hanging from his arm.

Willow and Crab reached the boat first. Good, she thought. Crab could help, and they could have the wing in place before Hazel and her knotting interfered. Lest the wing add too much weight to the boat, Willow said they should drag it closer to the water. "Let the front of it lie in the shallows," she said. "Then all that will be needed is a quick shove."

"Not too far in," Crab warned. "The water is rising."

"All the better," Willow responded. "You will not have to push too hard. As soon as I am in the boat, I will be away from here."

Crab hoisted the wing pole and set it in the socket. Then together they lashed it to the boat. Willow tugged each rope as tightly as she could. But when Crab, across from her, did the same, her side loosened. Crab had to remind her that the wing on Thorn's boat hadn't been entirely rigid either but could shift and bend with the boat.

At last they stood back to survey their work. The boat looked ready for launching. Now Willow could return to the huts for her pouch. She told Crab she would run both ways.

The dog raced to catch up with her. He had tried to follow Thorn into the sea. Maybe the dog sensed that she was leaving him too. If only she could bring him with her. But he might move when he should not, and he might add more weight than the boat could hold. That would be true of Crab as well. Still, Crab had never offered to join her. He couldn't know that she had thought of it. She would ask Crab to hold the dog as she set off. If he could.

Inside the passageway, she picked up the pouch she had set aside. She dug into it until her fingers reached the edge of the fire stone beside the hard strips of dried fish she had packed. That was all she needed to check.

"Willow!" Tall Reed's voice cut through the close air of the passageway. "Bring wood and turf to burn. Make haste. Why were you away again so early? Bring seal meat too. The uncles will be hungry."

Willow knew that if she didn't obey, she would arouse suspicion. Setting her pouch down beside a pile of driftwood, she stacked branches and sticks and carried them along the passageway, leaving a few at each hut's doorway. Back at the woodpile she hoisted heavier tree limbs. She had to make several trips through the passageway to satisfy Tall Reed, who came to inspect what she brought.

"Where is the seal meat?" the older woman demanded when Willow straightened as if the task were complete.

"Next," Willow mumbled. "It cannot all be done at once."

"I suppose the boys are not far. They might help."

Willow nodded. If she kept agreeing and obeying, maybe Tall Reed wouldn't turn her attention to the beach.

As Willow left, she paused at the stone basin outside the passageway to splash herself. But fresh cold water didn't remove the seal fat that could turn ropes slippery in her grasp. She held her hands out to the dog so that he could lick her fingers clean. Then she picked up her pouch and left.

5

Crab came running as though to meet her. But he didn't stop.

"Where are you going?" she called after him.

Without turning, he shouted back, "Tree boat."

She could only guess that her boat had drifted off the beach. How could he have let it float away? Maybe there had been some kind of distraction. Anyway, he was going for a tree boat and a paddle. He and Thistle should be able to catch any wayward basket-shaped boat with its wing wrapped around its pole.

She clambered up a dune to look for her boat. Adrift in the shallows, it bobbed aimlessly. Its wing, which had come loose from the pole, swung from side to side. Well, even so, the boat could still be retrieved. Crab would return with a tree boat and paddles. It wouldn't take long to catch her boat and beach it.

Thistle, knee-deep in the shallows, was shouting, "Keep down. Lie low." Gulls swooped and wailed overhead, their calls nearly drowning out his voice.

It wasn't until Willow had gained the beach that she fully realized her boat wasn't empty. A head poked up for an instant, Hazel's head. Willow wanted to shout to her to take hold of the rope attached to the wing. But even if Hazel could grab it, she wouldn't know what to do next. Thistle was right to tell her to lie low. At least then she would avoid being whacked as the wing swung above her.

"You should help Crab with the tree boat," Willow called to Thistle.

"He told me to stay, to keep talking to her," Thistle said.

"Well, I can do that. Get the tree boat." Later she would learn how the boys had let this come about. She already guessed that foolish Hazel had somehow caused the accident. "Keep your head down," Willow called over the water. "Do not move suddenly." Her voice rose. "Hazel, listen to me. Do not roll around in the boat. Stop!" By now Willow was shouting. "Stop flopping like a caught fish." What was the matter with that girl?

Crab and Thistle, with the tree boat between them, ran into the water. Crab held a paddle.

"Only one paddle?" Willow shouted.

Crab didn't answer. Thistle said, "I will need both hands to grab the boat and Hazel."

The tree boat, in pursuit of the drifting basket boat, skimmed across the water. Too fast. It couldn't be slowed before it rammed Willow's boat and set it spinning wildly. Hazel's head arose, then her shoulders, her arms flailing. Grasping at air, her hands made contact with the wing and held on. Only for an instant. Then the wing lifted her and flung her sideways. The boat dipped, tipping her out. Seawater gushed in.

It seemed to Willow on the beach that events raced and then slowed in terrifying sequence. Now the tree boat appeared to have been diverted. She could see Crab paddling furiously to straighten it. At the same time that Thistle's legs gripped the tree boat, his upper body and arms reached out to grab an exposed rock. This hindered Crab's efforts to make headway, and the tree boat was dragged sideways.

Meanwhile Hazel floundered in the kelp that floated around the seal ledges. She made no sound that Willow could hear. Her silence seemed to goad Thistle into frenzied contortions as he clung to the rock. Crab struggled to keep them afloat until Thistle was finally forced to release his grasp.

While the boys looked as though they opposed each other, it was clear that both were intent on rescuing Hazel. What Willow didn't realize at first was that they had abandoned her craft.

"My boat!" she shouted across the water. If the boys heard her, they made no attempt to respond. They were in pursuit of Hazel, who kept vanishing from sight and then emerging briefly before slipping once more beneath the kelp fronds.

Somehow Crab managed to gain enough control of the tree boat to nose it in through the ledges until Thistle could pull Hazel up and hold her limp body in front of himself.

Willow kept one eye on her foundering boat while she followed the tree boat's lumbering progress toward shore. She even steadied it as Crab thrust it onto the sand. Out by the ledges her escape boat seemed to come and go, wallowing fitfully, already sinking.

She held the tree boat so that Thistle could step free of it and pick up Hazel. The girl's blue-white skin and sagging mouth had the look of death. Aghast, Willow stared and then looked away. In that moment she lost track of her boat.

When she finally caught sight of it again, it was on its side, jammed between submerged rocks. As she watched, a young seal surfaced and poked the wing. Two more seals lunged at it, each a bit leery of what must seem part bird and part something strange. Then one of them tore the wing from its socket. For an instant the rounded basket lifted from the water. That was the last Willow saw of her boat before it was dragged down for good.

6

The gulls still shrieked. Thistle dragged Hazel onto dry sand and let go of her limp body. He looked up at Willow, then spoke hoarsely, as if he had also gulped too much seawater. "It was not safe, your craft. It wanted greater care in the making."

"Too late now," Willow retorted. "Since you let it go."

Thistle looked down at the motionless girl on the beach. That look was his reply.

Willow glanced at Crab, silently urging him to speak out. But Crab shook his head. He would stand with Thistle. Because he agreed that the boat was too hastily crafted? Because Hazel mattered more than any boat.

Bereft of her escape craft, it occurred to Willow that the uncles were bound to take her now. She leaned over Hazel's motionless body. A feeble sigh gurgled inside the slack mouth. She might not be dead after all. Willow squatted down, grabbed Hazel's shoulders, and turned her on her side.

"Leave her," Thistle commanded as water gushed out of Hazel. "You have done enough."

But Willow shook the girl. Water tinged with blood erupted in spurts. Then a faint whimper issued from Hazel's throat.

"Help!" Willow said to the boys. But neither of them knew what action should be taken now that Hazel seemed to be returning to life. So Willow simply held her, waiting for the outpouring to subside.

None of them heard Tall Reed approach until the woman came striding down from the last dune. "What have you done?" she demanded when she caught sight of Hazel on the beach. She elbowed Willow out of the way and bent over Hazel.

"Fetch Redstone and other strong uncles," Tall Reed told the boys.

Thistle didn't stir. He seemed unable to move from Hazel's side. But Crab started over the dunes in the direction of the huts.

Willow stepped back. Here was her pouch, made ready for the sea journey she would never take. But she might still be able to flee inland if she made her escape before the uncles arrived.

Willow hoisted up her pouch and ran after Crab. "I will leave now," she told him. "Even if Hazel lives, she may...may not be strong enough..."

"Where can you go?" Crab broke in. "They will find you."

"The other side of the valley of the trees," she said, beginning to pull ahead of him.

"No, Willow," he called to her. "The uncles themselves avoid that land. The Others will stop you with stones. That is why it is forbidden land."

Willow halted and faced him. "The Others never harmed Great Mother," she declared. "The Keeper of Story may go beyond ordinary limits. I will seek the path Great Mother used on her solitary journeys to find our stories."

"Stay," he implored. "The Others do not know you as Keeper of Story. What lies ahead here cannot be worse than wandering alone in a hostile land."

Willow shook her head. All she could say was, "Great Mother never feared the Others. She said a time would come when I would have to follow in her footsteps. This must be that time."

They parted before they had reached the hut cluster.

Willow clambered uphill, leaving the shell heap behind, leaving the smoke and the stirrings of morning with its warmth and food, leaving her father. Leaving Crab.

She was well on her way before thoughts and questions began to collect around her single impulse to flee. She had prepared for the sea. But here on land the uncles might track her down. Or would they expect her to return at day's end, just as she and the boys had done after each day of boatmaking? Surely for a while the uncles would be thinking only of Hazel. As for the boys, there was no telling what they would have to say about the failed boat.

But had it failed? What had possessed Hazel to climb inside to finish knotting the skin to the basketry? How could she have ignored the rocking of the boat as the tide lifted it free of land?

It should never have happened, Willow concluded. Hazel had been rash to get inside the boat, but the boys could have kept it safely beached. Had the water risen faster than usual? Well, maybe it hadn't been all that fast. Willow had stayed away longer than she intended because there had been a diversion, Tall Reed demanding that Willow attend to morning tasks. Was the loss of the boat due to this, or to Hazel's risking herself, or to the boys' inattention?

Did it matter anymore? Willow, so quick to blame her companions, decided that dwelling on faults, theirs or hers, wasted strength and purpose. All that mattered was that the boat was gone.

And now she, too, was gone, if she could reach the valley of trees ahead of any searchers. From there she would venture into the land beyond, the forbidden land from which no one but Great Mother had ever safely returned.

7

The clouds gathered and darkened. Then a fine rain began to fall. Willow allowed herself one blurry glimpse of the swamp pond where she had first tried her basket boat. She didn't dare stop. She needed to veer away from there to reach the valley. The farther she got this first day, the safer she would be, since no one would set out from the coast to look for her once this wet, gray day deepened into night.

But someone did pursue her. She sensed it before she could see or hear the person. As he gained ground, she started to run.

"No," shouted Crab. "Willow, wait."

Breathless, she paused to let him catch up. She saw that he carried a sack over his shoulder. Was he running away too?

"There is much confusion," he told her. "They are trying to rouse Hazel. She will not warm up. No one can tell what will become of her."

Willow didn't respond. She knew she would sound mean and uncaring if she spoke.

Crab handed over the sack. "You must take this with you," he said.

Willow hesitated. "Not if I am to cover great distances. I must move quickly." At least he no longer tried to stop her, to convince her to stay.

"You are not at sea," he declared. "There are no fish to catch in your little net. You will need what I have brought."

She gave in. Without asking what was inside the sack, she

slung it over her shoulder, her own pouch already hanging on the other one.

"How will the Others know you are the next Keeper of Story?" he asked.

"They will know," she told him, trying to sound more confident than she felt. "They know..." All at once she blurted, "Tell my father—"

"Tell him what?"

But her father would never understand why she had fled. "Tell him I seek our untold stories."

Crab nodded and turned to leave.

She watched him go, then suddenly called out to him. "*If* my father asks for me," she told Crab. "Tell him only if he asks."

She set off again, her steps less buoyant with the added weight of Crab's sack. After several paces more she halted and swiveled around again. As if sensing her gaze, Crab stopped and turned as well. She met his lingering look, but there was nothing else she could say.

She trudged along, determined to reach the valley of trees before night. The forbidden land that lay beyond must wait for daylight, for she would be far from the sea she knew and the flight for which she had prepared herself. She must not dwell upon the boat. It was lost. Nor could she think about Hazel, lost as well. Willow would banish regret.

When at last she came within sight of the trees, they seemed less imposing than before. When she had visited the valley with uncles and women, who had come to carry off trees for boats, the growing trees had towered overhead. Of course she herself had been smaller, and she had been listening to tales about the Others who lurked beyond the valley.

Great Mother had scoffed at those stories. "The People

of the Singing Seals make a muddle of events they fear," she had told Willow. "Long ago, when the sea rose up in one great Wave and drowned most of them, they were returning home with trees for boats. The few survivors were those who had lagged on the homeward journey. Because of the fearsome Wave, they or their children and their children's children falsely connect the valley of trees with any possible danger that might threaten them. It is for the Keeper of Story to part them from their nonsense tales, and that is not easily done. Or rather," Great Mother had added with a chuckle, "it is not hard for the Keeper to tell what is true. It is hard for the uncles and women to accept either uncertainty or knowledge."

Willow could almost hear Great Mother's calm, even voice. It reminded her that she must attend to her own needs while a trace of light remained. After this long, wet trek inland, Willow knew that once she dropped her pouch and sack, her shoulders and legs would feel the strain. Without rest, they might even fail her when she set out tomorrow.

The rain had long since given way to a fine mist. Even if Willow could make a spark here, there would be no dry tinder to feed a fire. All that remained then was to settle down wet for the night and refresh herself with something to eat. But she was thirsty. She had packed dried fish because she had assumed she could collect rainwater in the boat.

She seated herself on a patch of moss, her back against the crusty tree trunk, and dug into Crab's sack. The first thing she pulled from it was a sheepskin cover. Next came a bundle of rawhide strips, and after that a small pack wrapped in bird skin containing a dense lump that might be food. In the waning light she couldn't be sure what it was, so she reached more deeply into the sack to extract what remained: a claw, seal teeth, two hoofed leg bones with smoked meat attached, and a large clamshell for digging.

She pondered this collection of Crab's belongings. Had he made them ready in case he might join her in the boat? Or had he packed them for her in haste while her absence went unnoticed and he was still able to carry them to her?

Grateful for the sheepskin, she spread it and then rolled herself inside it. She landed on her back, staring up at the darkening sky and the overhanging fretwork of trees. The bare branches creaked ominously, bending and then clenching as if to grasp at prey. These trees belonged to a world as different from hers as the sea was from the land.

She had no choice but to unwind herself from the cover and move. She dragged the sheepskin and everything else out in the open where nothing swung above her. But here the wind flogged her. She stumbled about, groping in the dark, until she came to a boulder that provided a bit of shelter on its downwind side. Once again she began to wrap herself in the sheepskin.

That was when the small pouch tumbled out of Crab's sack. She felt the thin wrapping and found an edge she could peel. The haunting aroma of slightly rancid berries came rising up from her fingers. These tightly packed berries could have been the very ones she herself had picked. She nibbled and then allowed herself one big bite before wrapping them and thrusting the dense pack inside the smaller pouch.

Now she was truly hungry, so she gnawed the sheep bone. Gulping down some of the stringy meat, she resisted the temptation to reopen the berry pack. She wondered if Crab had guessed how much his gift would mean to her.

She stretched out, turning on her stomach to shield her

face from falling mist. But she still felt exposed, so she curled up to make herself small enough to be entirely covered.

Even so, unfamiliar sounds filled her with unease. She told herself they were probably caused by gusts of mist blown down from nearby trees. She would not allow any false or foolish meaning to attach itself to those sounds, for she knew perfectly well that the wind moaned and the trees still creaked, whether or not she lay beneath them.

8

In her sleep she was rocking. That had to mean that she was in her boat. She had only dreamed that it was lost and that she had fled inland. Great Mother used to say that dreams might be warnings. Was Willow being warned that the boat was unready, Hazel at risk? Later, Willow thought. Later she would recover her dream of Hazel and the lost boat. For now she clung to this buoyancy and knew that she was held and warm.

Much later, still wrapped in darkness, she began to awaken. She pressed against the pliant sheepskin and felt pressure return. Her fingers crept to her face to shove aside the top of her cover. Only then did she open her eyes. Gray, watery light. The sea? No, her dream of being waterborne had dissolved, and she could tell that she was grounded. She stretched and pushed again. Now she felt resistance. Something at her back held for an instant, then yielded. There was a soft grunt, an extravagant yawn.

She knew the sound. She recognized the pressure. She pulled herself partly free of the sheepskin wrap so that she could turn and look. Here he was, Thorn's dog, his crumpled ear hard against her neck. Her joy erupted in laughter. The dog's tail thumped the ground, stirring up bits of grass.

The morning's dull light gleamed with promise. Maybe that light would make itself felt before night forced it to retreat. The sun might even dry off the sodden land.

Willow was eager to start her journey out of the valley, especially now with the dog at her side. But he left her to pursue something that rustled among the trees. She packed up her pouch and sack and watched him leap, curving airborne as he pounced upon some small prey she couldn't see. It was barely in his mouth and gulped down before he leaped again, and then again.

When at last he stopped and looked around, she guessed he wanted water. Maybe if they got started now they would find some soon. But he wouldn't leave the trees without pursuing the next tiny beast he came upon. This one he carried to Willow and dropped at her feet. A vole. She picked it up. She would carry it for him. There was no telling what he would find to eat after they left the valley of trees.

But he still couldn't resist the ready prey and kept catching more voles and bringing them to Willow, who had to stop and tuck each one away in her pouch against a possible lean time to come.

9

Where the trees ended and the land sloped upward into a strengthening wind, Willow paused to prepare herself for what lay beyond. The Others. Great Mother had believed that Willow would soon be ready for the truth about them. It must follow what she learned about the Wave that once overwhelmed the People of the Singing Seals and the changes it brought to them. To prepare Willow for this truth, Great Mother had told of shadow shapes and the stories they contained. And always, beneath and above these stories, reared Star the Boundless. Again and again Great Mother had related his seafaring story, his journey through time.

Willow strode up the incline to cast her eyes over undulating heath that so resembled her own land near the coast that for a moment she thought her eyes tricked her. Only the light was different, that and no worn paths to follow.

Now that she had quit the enclosed valley, there was nothing to break the long sweep of wind that coursed across the turf grasses, stinging her face and causing her eyes to tear. She glanced down at the dog beside her. Had he ever come this far with his own pack when they disappeared from the coast for days? Would he lead her to a stream or pond?

But the dog didn't take the lead. He simply stood while she surveyed the low hills that seemed to stretch to the rising sun itself. There was no sign of the Others. Willow had expected to see their deadly stones piled and ready to be cast at anyone who set foot on their land.

She stepped forward and set her direction at an angle

from the valley so that the wind now swept in at her side. Great Mother must have walked this way, thought Willow.

The dog kept pace with her, his head low as if he sought a familiar scent. The grass, still green but with bleached flecks, was only now turning brown. Off in the distance grazing beasts raised their heads to stare at the girl and the dog. Sheep? No, deer. More curious than fearful, they soon dropped their heads to the grass again.

The dog eyed them but didn't even stiffen. Now that he was full of voles, thought Willow, he wasn't inclined to chase after bigger prey. Then he sniffed the air and set off at a trot, veering off from Willow's direction and turning away from the distant grazers, away from the wind.

Guessing that he smelled water, she tried to keep up with him. But her pouch and sack weighed her down, and she fell behind.

He disappeared down a slope, then emerged on the next rise. "Wait," she called to him.

But on he went. All she could do was hope for glimpses of him every time he reached higher ground. With mounting irritation she recalled how he'd always responded promptly to Thorn's commands. But then so did the seals when Thorn called them to shore. If only she had learned how to speak with beasts.

Great Mother had often said that you cannot learn more than one thing at a time. Willow should learn each thing well before turning to another or attempting to build upon stories so new to her that they could not yet become memory. Such stories were too raw to blend with the Story that would take Willow a lifetime to acquire. So start at the beginning, she would remind Willow, at the beginning, which is the journey of Star the Boundless.

Only now, with Great Mother gone, Willow summoned a kind of defense of herself. At least she had learned how to craft a seaworthy boat. Nearly.

She wondered how Thorn would have regarded her finished craft. Crab and Thistle had pronounced the making too hasty. Were they right? Had she been so driven to complete it that she had been careless? If so, it only confirmed Great Mother's view, and Thistle had reason to blame Hazel's accident on Willow.

But she had warned herself against dwelling on the boat and Hazel. What mattered now was keeping track of the dog and finding water. There he was again, smaller in the distance. He had covered more ground.

The hoarse croak of an unseen raven mocked her unanswered call, a second raven promptly responding. Its voice rasped through the morning as it tumbled into view. Then, breaking its fall, it soared skyward again, wing feathers spread like black fingers clawing the thin gray air.

Watching it, she could almost feel the loft of its flight. Surely that was how she would have felt in her boat once it had cleared the ledges and carried her onto the open sea. Everything seemed to hurl her thoughts back to the boat.

She continued on. Hunger and thirst drove her as well as an uneasiness she couldn't identify. Not fear exactly. She wondered how she would find her way back to the valley of trees if she ever did decide to return to her people. She kept glancing over her burdened shoulder. The treetops were no longer visible. She tried to check her direction by the source of the blurred sunlight, but she couldn't be sure of it.

Keep the dog in sight. Press forward.

10

When Willow lost all contact with the dog, she had to fight off the urge to retrace her steps and return to the valley of trees. She doubted she would have felt this lost alone on the pathless sea. The boat would have carried her away from land. She assumed it would have headed like Thorn's boat, not just away, but toward, toward the edge of the visible world where the sun always sets before oncoming night. This much she had believed and expected. Venturing beyond the valley of trees was something she had never imagined.

She wished she had considered the possibility of land flight. She couldn't even recover a few scraps from Great Mother's brief reflections on her solitary journeys. Any accounts that Willow was able to recall scattered in disarray before the brutal fact of utter strangeness.

After she admitted to herself that she had lost sight of the dog, she stopped and let her pouch and sack slide to the ground. Then she sat down, stretched her legs out, and leaned back. She knew that food would boost her hopes and her determination to escape the life her father and the uncles demanded of her. She should not return, especially now that Hazel's condition was in doubt. The uncles might even be tempted to give Willow to Twin Trunk Tree.

Willow sat up, rummaged in her pouch, and brought out the berry pack. She allowed herself a nibble. As on the night before, she yielded to the rush of hunger and chewed some of the smoked meat from the leg bone. Shadows alerted her to the sudden approach of buzzards circling overhead. How quickly and silently they had appeared. Did it mean that this was a hungry land? She thought of the voles in Crab's pack. When she rose to continue on her journey, she left two of the small dead creatures on the ground behind her.

On her way again, she glanced back to see the buzzards and an array of crows scaling down to the ground, the crows more agile but too leery of the buzzards to contest the found prey.

She began to stumble as she descended another hill. Her eyes were on the distance ahead, and it wasn't until she glanced down at her feet that she realized that the ground banked as though deliberately cut and shaped into long, sloping steps. It came to her that at home after certain storms, the seabed descended like this from the shallows to the depths. What kind of storm could produce this shelving effect on the land?

She was still puzzling over this when she sensed that she wasn't alone. First she went still. Then, feeling a presence behind her, above her, she slowly turned. Two dogs. No, three. They must have been tracking her since she left the voles on the ground. She could tell at once that they didn't belong to the home pack. Those dogs had learned to keep their distance from people. These three, perhaps emboldened by hunger, eyed her with keen interest. The largest one moved away from the other two, toward Willow.

She knew better than to encourage them with offerings of voles. She didn't doubt that they could smell the tiny beasts. Probably they smelled the sheep leg too. But she shouldn't turn her back on them either.

She decided she had no choice but to face them, to force them to back off or else to pass her. She walked up the incline, her eyes staring into those of the biggest dog, the one that had stepped toward her. He uttered a low warning growl as she approached. She stopped to give him space to turn and leave her. At first he held his ground. Then he turned sideways and walked carefully around her. The other two dogs took his place.

Surrounded, she faced them fully. Then she stomped uphill, passing between them, and continued on for another few paces before turning back to confront all three of them.

The lead dog seemed unsettled now. He swung his head slowly from side to side. She should have something to throw at him, but the only stone she carried was the precious fire stone. Slowly she reached into her pouch. Her fingers closed around the berry pack. She aimed for the dog's head and hurled the pack. He dodged as it came at him, but it dealt him a blow to the shoulder. He uttered a muted yelp. The other two sprang away as if they had been struck as well.

Now that Willow had the advantage over them, she couldn't think what to do next. She wanted them to retreat down the slope so that she could keep the advantage of height. She wanted to retrieve the berry pack before it was lost to the dogs or scavenging birds. But she had to maintain her stance. If she could force them to back away from her and then give them space enough to turn, maybe they would leave her.

With her eyes still fastened on the lead dog, she swung Crab's sack ahead of her and strode purposefully toward them. Maybe the swinging sack was too threatening, for all three dogs slunk off. She watched them trot close together, heads and tails low, ears back.

As she picked up the berry pack and stuffed it into the

sack, it occurred to her that this small pack of wild dogs seemed to be going in the same direction that Thorn's dog had taken. She was reluctant to follow, but she needed to find him. They needed to stick close together.

11

Willow could feel her strength drain away. She plodded along, increasingly aware of the weight she carried. She tried to concentrate on the uneven ground underfoot.

On the crest of another hill she paused to gaze ahead. The sameness of turf and browning grasses, still beaded with moisture, stretched away on either side. But partly hidden below the next hillock a different surface glared darkly. It could be stone, she told herself. Wet stone might glint like water, especially if the low sun was too weak to burn off last night's mist.

If it was part of a rocky outcrop, it might be where the wild dogs denned. She approached slowly, taking care to notice anything that moved on or near that gleaming gray. Descending into the lowland before the hill, she splashed between tussocks, peaty brown water rising over her feet. She longed to kneel here and drink. But she would be too vulnerable, especially if the dogs were just over the next rise.

Leaning into this hill, she lost sight of the gray glint. She forced herself to lengthen her strides until she gained enough height to see that the hillock flattened on its farther side. She saw no rock, no den. But just beyond the shallow slope a dark pool spread before her. Thorn's dog was there, belly-deep in the water, the biggest wild dog confronting him.

Shrugging off her pouch and pack and then beginning to swing the pack as she had done before, she splashed toward them. She shouted too. The big dog turned his head, only for an instant, but long enough. Thorn's dog plunged past him onto the boggy heath where the two other dogs crouched.

Hackles raised along his neck and back, Thorn's dog walked past them, then continued on around the low margin of the pool until he reached Willow.

Placing himself in front of her, he pressed against her legs and stared across the pool at the lead dog. Willow could feel a growl vibrate through his body, but she heard nothing. He remained like that until the lead dog and the other two turned and walked away.

Before Willow descended to the pool, she unloaded two more voles. The dog took them in two swift gulps, then followed her to the water. She drank and drank, ignoring the wetness that crept up her tunic. She supposed she would be cold now, but all she could do was slake her thirst. Whatever came next would be bearable once she had her fill.

What came next was dried fish, which she tried to chew slowly, savoring the saltiness now that she could drink as much as she wanted. The dog sat and watched her until finally she couldn't bear his eyes on her and gave up the last of the voles. "Now you will have to hunt," she told him. At the sound of her voice, he cocked his lopsided head. His look reminded her that Thorn spoke with the beasts in song and silence. Not exactly song, she thought, but not the usual word sounds that people made.

"You will hunt," she said, "and I will make you understand, and then you will not leave me again."

The dog stood up, shook himself, and glanced off in the direction of the wild dogs. Then he lay down, his eyes on Willow's face. It crossed her mind that he might prefer to follow them, possibly even join their group if they would allow it. How could he know that she couldn't tame them? Only Thorn had such power.

"So do not leave me," she said to him before crouching to drink again.

Almost at once she began to shiver. She pulled out the sheepskin cover and slung it over herself. Then she loosened the soaked tunic and stepped out of it. Spreading it to dry on the stiff moor grasses, she cast her eyes about her, seeking any sign of exposed peat to use in case she was able to start a small fire with brittle heather stems.

But everything was too wet, and she had only the shell for digging. And no sign of ready peat to burn. So she clutched the sheepskin tightly around herself until the dog rose with a sigh and walked over to her. She opened the cover and then brought it around them both. He groaned with resignation and settled beside her, his own warmth gradually spreading through to her. Slowly her shivering subsided.

When she drew back the cover to release him, she found that her tunic was almost as wet as when she had spread it out. All she could do was roll it up and stuff it in Crab's sack. She would walk on with the cover held about her, an awkward arrangement while hauling her pouch and the sack, but preferable to wearing the saturated tunic.

The dog regarded her expectantly, almost eagerly. He had known where to find water. Maybe he knew something else that lay ahead. Not the three dogs, she thought, but something like shelter or prey to sustain them both.

"Don't leave me," she demanded as he set off at a trot, the distance between them already beginning to lengthen.

He didn't even glance back. But his good ear flicked, this tiny signal informing her that he had heard. What he understood or intended might yet be revealed. For now all she could do was try to keep up with him as picked his way over the heath. She kept alert, though, in case the three wild dogs or any others should ambush them.

Ahead, the dog maintained a steady, purposeful pace, almost as if he knew where he was or where he was heading.

For Willow the landscape seemed featureless. The low mounds and hillocks, lacking shadows, were somehow all alike beneath the sullen light of the shielded sun.

12

Near the close of the brief day, Willow found herself lagging even farther behind the dog. The wind, unchecked, stung her eyes; just keeping him in sight seemed too much of an effort. It was up to him, not to her, whether he left her or stayed close. Either way, she would soon be caught by darkness.

If only she could find some outcrop for shelter. While the dimming gray light remained, she cast her tearing eyes over the undulating land. What crossed her line of sight was the dog. He bounded off so suddenly and with such swiftness that in the next instant he was lost to her. She stopped at once. There was nothing to be gained by continuing on. She would use the last of the light to gather heather stems, as many as she could pick, for the wind had finally scoured them dry. She would make a spark, and then she would feed it with every brittle plant she could find.

But the wind scattered her stems. She made a windbreak out of her wet tunic and her pouch. She must be careful, she warned herself, lest she set the wrong thing ablaze. She could almost hear Thorn warning her against haste. So what would he do? He would use the shell. He would dig an earthen pit to shelter a spark and only then coax it into a flame.

She heard the panting dog approach. At the same time she smelled blood. Then she felt his warm sides heaving as he stood next to her. Something flopped down in front of him. He nudged it at her. But she couldn't turn from the dried stems she was rubbing just as they were heating up. Bending over to enclose them, she intensified the friction. Yes, they smoked. Harder and harder she rubbed, and then just when she thought the smoke was dying, a tiny orange eye blinked open and then shut. She tried to blow it into life again.

She started over. But after the next spark appeared, she couldn't reach the prepared stems. She groped frantically, then guessed that they must be under the dog. She plunged her hand under his belly and withdrew a fistful of stems.

Just as the spark threatened to go out, she made her first flame. She fed it with another stem and then another. In her haste she overloaded the little fire with too many stems and nearly killed it.

The dog backed away, releasing more stems. She made herself slow down as she added them. The flame was fuller now, giving off the scent of heat, the promise of warmth, and a flicker of light as well. That light showed her the hare that the dog had killed and brought to her. She guessed that he must have flipped it to break its neck, for the only visible blood was a drop from its nose. She glanced from hare to dog and saw that his forepaws and chest were smudged with blood. She guessed he had killed another hare and eaten it. This one really was for her, then. But she had no way to skin it and sustain the fire at the same time.

Frantically she tore more heather from the turf, this time by the roots. She was adding these to the little flame when she noticed the attached soil. It was brown and peaty. The flame sputtered and then surged. More roots, she thought, moving far enough off to find a fresh patch to pull. She knew that the damp roots might put out her fire, but they were all the tinder at hand.

Once she had an ample supply of dried grass and heather beside the fire, she turned her attention to the hare. She was determined not to damage the pelt. Its soft white fur retained a few faded brown splotches. Had it lived, it would have turned all white by the first big snowfall.

She fetched out the fire stone to make the first long cut. Then she rummaged in her pouch for the sharp seal tooth set in bone that could slice sinew and nip flesh. All the while she kept an eye on her fire. Before she could slip the carcass from its skin, she had to stop to replenish her tinder.

She used the fire stone again, this time to suspend the hare over the flame. The seal tooth with its bone handle served as an opposite support. She had to keep positioning these props, especially after the carcass began to drip onto the fire. She needed more hands to fuel the flame while she turned the meat.

The dog watched her frantic efforts. Every time she scorched her fingers and gasped with pain and annoyance, he drew back as if he feared that her displeasure was aimed at him.

Finally she let the seared meat drop. The fire hissed, smoked, and sank in upon itself. Only then did the dog relax and attend to his own cleanup. She could hear his rhythmic licking until her chewing and crunching shut out everything but the sound of her own bliss.

13

The following days fell into a pattern of walking and hunting and stopping to eat. Willow would have been glad to dig out a shelter beside one of the streams or pools where they paused to drink. But the dog seemed driven. He behaved as if he knew where he was heading. She had no say in the matter. Not only did he provide food for them both, but he kept her from freezing at night when the wind flayed the turf with ice.

Once they caught sight of the three wild dogs on the horizon, but she and the dog continued on their course and there was no confrontation. Or else these were other wild dogs. Willow guessed that the three that had challenged her and Thorn's dog must have split off from a larger pack.

Now that she knew she could dig for peat, she tried to dry some. But she never remained anywhere under the sun long enough to turn it into useful tinder. Besides, when they stopped to sleep, the wind either scattered her supply or froze it.

She kept looking for ledge or outcrops where she might find shelter for a sustained fire, but so far this land appeared to be as devoid of stone as it was empty of Others. She thought longingly of the hare pelt, but there was never any daylight left to work it when they stopped for the night. So she carried it and the next one the dog brought, imagining covers for her hands. She would find a way to make them as soon as the pelt became supple.

Once the dog came trotting to her carrying a duck with a broken wing—a rare find, since ducks usually disappeared in the dark season. When she pitched it, scorched, from the fire to the ground, the dog moved close. She cut it in half and placed the two portions side by side. He approached hesitantly, then picked up what was nearest him and took it away to eat. When he remained where he had eaten, she took the rest of the duck and began her own meal.

Before they resumed their journey, she gathered the few feathers scattered about. She wondered whether she had been too hasty in letting most of them burn. She longed for a hood for her head. She would attach it to her tunic to protect her neck from the biting wind. If she could.

Only now did she realize she should have brought a stitching bone, one end pointed, the other blunt with a hole for attaching gut or braided grass. If the dog made another kill, she would save some bones and insides and then try to recall how to make one herself.

She no longer worried when the dog ran off. He always returned, even without a kill. So when he bolted suddenly, she kept on in the direction they had been heading, her mind sorting through the process that turned ordinary bones into stitching tools. Reluctantly she reminded herself of Thorn's insistence on braiding fibers to make them stronger than single strands. Then she couldn't help thinking of the ropes she had braided for her boat.

Lost in thought, she gazed out across the sloping heath. What she saw stopped her in her tracks. Way ahead stretched a line of trees, only not like those in the valley. These were stripped of their branches, like tree boats in the making. Yet different. They were all still upright.

She glanced around, hoping to catch sight of the dog returning from his hunt. She didn't know whether to wait for him or go on. They would stop soon if he brought prey to her. But if he didn't, she would have to keep going.

Even when she was well fed, the thought of a stop for fire and sizzling meat was a powerful lure, disrupting thoughts of tools and their use and filling her with a different kind of hunger—for her own bed closet and the hut fire and ample portions of seal and sheep and, nearby, the hush or roar of the sea.

The dog caught up with her, panting hard and without prey. She could tell there had been a hard chase. His tongue lolled, and his muzzle was beaded with droplets from his own breath. She would have been glad to stop for a rest, but he seemed intent on pressing forward. She couldn't tell whether he noticed the massive tree trunks in the distance. He just kept heading in their direction.

It took a while for her to see what they really were. Not trees at all, but upright stones that looked as if an array of gigantic beings had turned to stone. Maybe these were the Others. Maybe they hadn't confronted Willow when she left the valley because they had become frozen like this, transformed. Willow stared at them, glanced down at the dog, and stared some more.

Snow filled the air and swirled on sudden updrafts as if rising from the turf. Of course this was the beginning of the cold time, so snow wasn't unexpected. Still, she dreaded the drifts that might build up in the wind and conceal hollows or rocky outcrops that could provide shelter.

The dog kept going. Willow squinted to shut out the snow as she set her eyes on the standing stones. They seemed to be moving toward her and the dog. Could they walk? The snow blotted them from her sight and then blew off enough for her to see once again. They seemed to have come closer. Yet each time she fixed them with her gaze, they stood unmoving in a great circle that seemed to describe a full moon or the sun at its height.

14

Even through driving snow, Willow could see the dog's hackles rise, the hairs along his neck and shoulders turned to icy barbs. He swerved onto a lower curve of land. That left her standing on the berm that surrounded the stone circle.

She thought of the uneven ground she had trod since emerging from the valley. As soon as she had realized that this land pattern resembled the coastal seabed, she had been able to look for it ahead. Shadows had helped, but they were rare, and those curving ramparts tended to lose their distinctive shape as the gentle hills absorbed them.

Here, though, the earthen ring surrounding the enormous stones was clearly defined. The upright stones themselves, lodged in higher ground, would dwarf the tallest of uncles. As far as she could see through the snow, no marks were incised on their rough surface. So what were they? Who were they?

She glanced around for the dog but couldn't see him. The snow was already mounting where the land stepped. She felt cold at her core. She had known this feeling only once before, on her last morning with the boat.

It came to her that this cold might be a kind of fear, something she usually recognized only in others. In the past she had tended to mock the fearful, until Great Mother had put an end to that. Mockery, she informed Willow, was a weapon to be used but rarely. Willow had a deal more living to get through before she would be ready to recognize the need for such a weapon. Then and only then might she resort to mockery.

Willow brushed off her bare legs. The dog emerged through the baffle of snow, a snow dog himself until he shook. He nudged her and started off again. She scrambled to keep him in sight and then to keep up with him. All the while she kept wondering about those massive stones and the danger they harbored. She had to trust the dog even though the stones seemed to have lured him into their presence. Why then had he shunned them so abruptly?

She followed him into the swirling snow that removed all shape and contour from the land. Nothing was certain but that this white sameness rendered her as helpless as if she were forging through absolute darkness.

Could the dog sense her dread of losing him? He seemed to have slowed. Then he veered off in what she guessed was a new direction. Instead of blasting her in the face, the wind-driven snow now buffeted her. Then it thrust her forward, causing her to lurch more often and to flounder. Each time she lost her balance, the dog appeared at once, although he vanished as quickly, before she had a chance to brush off snow from her legs, her pack, her pouch.

The snow even consumed the dog. She imagined walking alone like this forever. The effort and her sightlessness drained all understanding and left nothing to remind her of why she was here and what she might hope for. Only the wind propelled her.

And then, all at once, the wind ceased. She staggered into a covered place without snow, and there she stopped. It smelled foul. It reeked of rot.

She rubbed the snow from her face and looked around. Sheltering rock. Beasts had already used it for a den. Something in its dark interior dripped. She was too exhausted to investigate. She just lowered her pouch and pack, pulled them back from the opening, and continued to stand. She couldn't think how to make her legs bend or her arms support her.

The dog nosed the pouch. He wanted the last of the dried fish. The pouch was frozen shut, her fingers too stiff to open it. Gradually it came to her that if she could remove the partly dried sheepskin, it could warm her. But she didn't move. Another thought formed inside her head. If those stones were frozen people from long ago, maybe she was becoming stone, too.

After a while she became aware of the dog panting. He was with her. He had brought her here. Slowly thoughts of standing stones receded. She began to recall the valley of trees and the berry pack and the ravens and buzzard and hares and the broken-winged duck. The three wild dogs.

Gradually more thoughts gathered and arranged themselves into a kind of understanding. She had left the warmth and safety of home to escape the only life she would be allowed there. Now she was cold and tired and wet. She was here, nowhere, and she was alone but for the dog. Still, she was beyond the uncles' reach, so in a sense she wasn't as lost as she would have been if she had stayed.

Stiffly she bent to the pouch. At first she couldn't feel anything. Then it took her a long time to pry the rawhide strips apart from the dried fish. She allowed herself one bite, then handed the rest to the dog. He gulped it down, then regurgitated and ate it again. His chomping sounded as though he were chewing ice.

The one frozen bite she had taken remained in her mouth. She wouldn't swallow it yet, not until she could taste it.

15

Willow awoke when the dog crept out from under the sheepskin. She opened her eyes and shut them quickly against the dazzle of light that angled into the den. Then she rolled onto the warm space left by the dog.

The next thing she knew, he was pawing at her. The sharp light had softened; it was more diffuse now and easier on her eyes. The dog pawed until she propped herself up. As soon as she was sitting on bare stone, she began to think about making a fire.

"Stay here," she pleaded. "It can be our home for a while."

The dog walked to the opening, lifted his leg, and peed against the entrance stone.

At once her own need to relieve herself forced her up and out. Then she surveyed their surroundings. She was looking down from halfway up a slope. Overnight the wind had blown the snow from higher elevations like this den. But at the lower level the snow had been driven into strange landforms, some like curving waves, some like the lumpish great-toothed seal that occasionally appeared offshore at home.

She ducked back inside the shelter, quickly casting her eyes about her. But the contrast with the brilliance outside turned everything dark. She waited for sight to return, then wrapped her feet in the sealskin boots. Even drenched, they would provide some protection against the sodden land she would soon be treading.

Peering closely at the den floor, she found nothing she or the dog could eat. But there was a small heap of stones close to one inner wall. What kind of beast piled stones like that? What were they for? Her gaze followed the rough surface of the wall up to the capstone. She couldn't tell whether this formation was an accident of time and weather or the product of invention and labor.

Water dripped from melting snow that had sifted down, and clumps of lichen furred the rock face. There seemed to be faint markings, barely visible on the uneven stone. Maybe they formed shadow beasts, but she couldn't be sure. Knowing how she tended to find stories within ordinary events, she supposed she might see design where there was none.

She would have crept into the deeper recess of the shelter to look for whatever else might be found, but the dog remained outside and she could feel his impatience. Reluctantly she gathered up her belongings and joined him out in the dazzling day.

At once he rose and trotted down the slope toward the snow shapes. Then he halted. The three wild dogs emerged from behind a drift. They gazed at Willow and the dog, then beyond them at the den. Their den? If so, they hadn't yet asserted their right to it.

Thorn's dog led Willow around the side of the hill. She glanced back. The three wild dogs hadn't moved. She thought of them reclaiming their den and wondered what they would make of the scents she and Thorn's dog had left there.

As the sun rose higher, the snow thinned, leaving the hilltops mottled green and brown and white. And gray. For at last rocky outcrops appeared among the steeper hills.

The dog kept to the high land. She assumed this was to extend his view of small prey venturing into the open. Twice he pounced on voles or mice. She couldn't be sure which they were because he swallowed them at once. She tried not to think about food, although she gazed longingly at a small lake just below them where she might find fish. But she didn't dare set off on her own.

When the dog paused, sniffing and staring down the slope toward the lake, she followed his gaze until she caught sight of tumbled blocks of snowy turf. Her first thought was that some beast had dug into the ground, dislodging earthen lumps. But what kind of beast could pile up that much debris? The snow blotted out the extent of the heap, but she guessed that it joined some natural landform.

The dog turned and started down. Willow was elated. While he nosed around, she could drag her net in the lake and maybe catch a few fish. As he descended, he edged away from the turf heap, stopping to sniff the air. She chafed at his caution, but she didn't push past him.

All at once he crouched. Willow followed his gaze to the lake. From there a furred head emerged, and then a long dark body further elongated by its tail. At the edge of the lake this beast had to break through ice that rimmed the shore. Clamped between its jaws flapped a fish, which it didn't pause to eat. Instead it flowed over the snowy bank, its body looping high and low.

Just as the dog sprang to intercept the leaping beast, it occurred to Willow that it must be an otter. She had seen one only once after the home pack had torn it apart, but afterward Great Mother had described otters she occasionally saw on her extended rambles. They didn't usually venture near the People of the Singing Seals, although whether because of the People or the home dog pack Great Mother couldn't say.

Now here came this beast, as flowing and graceful as a

porpoise. Thorn's dog was bearing down on it when a stone came hurtling through the air, striking the dog's neck. He yelped but kept on. A second stone struck harder. This time the dog grunted and fell onto his side.

Willow saw someone draped in tattered skins step closer and take aim with yet another stone. She shrieked at him to stop. Startled, the stone thrower glanced her way. The dog crept back toward Willow. The otter bolted with its fish.

16

Stunned to see a living person here, Willow gaped at him.

He looked old and thin, and his eyes peered at her out of sunken sockets. He wore a small pack on his back. She guessed it carried stones like the one he still held. When she saw that he meant to finish off the dog, she shook her head and flung her arms around the dog. He winced in pain.

The ragged old man stared at the girl and the dog. He said, "My otter. My fish. You cannot stay, or otter comes no more."

Willow could barely understand him. She said, "We did not know. I will catch more fish for all of us."

"Girl," said the man. He shook his head. "Too late, you."

"Too late for what?" Willow asked him.

"Too late to give back. Too late."

Willow struggled to understand. Did he mean too late to give back the fish? "Maybe not too late," she offered.

"Or else too early," the old man told her.

Too late. Too early. She supposed he must have lost his wits. But what if he hadn't? "Too late or too early?" she asked. "It cannot be both at once."

The old man leaned toward her and spoke very slowly. "Girl, you. Too late if your people send you. Too early if you be next Keeper of Story." Then he added, "She comes no longer, Keeper."

"You mean Great Mother?" Willow asked him.

"Aah," moaned the man.

At a loss, Willow tried to reach him another way. "I have a net for fish. Do you have fire?"

The ragged old man nodded and turned away from her. Only then did she see that the tumbled turf behind him was a kind of hut, its doorway a gaping mouth that swallowed him up. Shrugging off her pack and pouch, she rummaged for the net. When she headed for the lakeshore, the dog came limping with her.

She tore off her boot skins and plunged through ice into the water. Gasping from the shock of cold, she tottered over stones and thrust the net below the surface. She knew she should take time to catch a small fish to lure bigger ones, but she couldn't resist the little fish swimming every which way around her legs. So she caught one, tossed it onto the bank, and greedily went after another. She repeated this until she realized that the dog was gobbling every small fish she tossed his way.

She forced herself to slow down. She captured one small fish and then weighted the net with a stone so that she could drag the net at just the right depth to entice larger fish. The moment two at once swam in after the live bait, she scooped up both.

She scrambled barefoot over snow and rocks and turf to the hut. "Fish," she called into the dark interior.

The old man stepped out and seized the fish.

She ran back to the lake to try again. Two or three more fish of that size, and there would be enough with maybe something to save for the next hunger. Despite the icy grip of the water, she managed to stay upright. She was thankful that there was no wave action in this lake, no sea force sucking debris from beneath her.

She was satisfied with just one more fish, since it was even larger than the last two. Besides, the icy water was robbing her of quickness and balance and she was fumbling like Hazel.

She let the dog sniff her catch but held it aloft so that he would understand that this one was not for him. At least not yet.

As she approached the turf hut with her catch, smoke issued from within, some of it winding upward through an unseen gap in the roof, and some filling the opening and spreading before her.

"More fish," she called as she blinked away tears. She went as close as she could without entering. The dog stood behind her.

The man stepped through the doorway. When he caught sight of the dog, he shook his head and gestured harshly as if to hurl another stone.

"He helps me," Willow said. "You must not hurt him, and he will not hurt you."

The man eyed the dog warily as he reached for the fish. Then he turned with an abrupt gesture of invitation to her and withdrew inside the dark hut.

Willow hesitated. If he meant that only she might come to his fire, maybe she should refuse. But the smell of burning peat combined with roasting fish was too enticing to resist. She touched the dog's head before she went inside. She hoped he would stay close.

She had to stoop as she entered. She felt her way along the inside wall. But as she gained a sense of the space and moved closer to the fire, she found she could stand upright.

At first all she could see was one overhead crack of light with smoke drawn into it. The smoke that filled the doorway blocked most of the daylight that might have allowed her to examine this man's living space, but she did catch a glimpse of a stone heap like the one in the rock shelter. That could mean there were more of his kind nearby.

"Where are the rest of your people?" she asked as she crouched before the fire. Pain shot up through her warming feet and ankles. She shifted her weight to ease the pressure. She tried to cup her toes in her hands but fell sideways. The fire sputtered as ash and peat dust shot up. The two fish on the embers swelled and then sank.

Groping through a small collection of bones at her feet, Willow found a deer antler prong, which she used to pry out the two fish before the fire consumed them. The old man knelt across from the low flame. He was still holding her last catch. Slowly he lowered it onto the fire, which hissed and then flared.

Willow scooped up one of the cooked fish and handed it over to him. He retreated into the darkness with it. Like a dog, thought Willow—a dog removing its prey from any who might challenge it. She heard his quick, in-drawn breath and guessed that he had burned his fingers or tongue.

"Where are your people?" she asked again. Carefully she lifted the skin of her fish and drew the half-cooked flesh from the bone. She couldn't eat it slowly, couldn't keep from gobbling. Still, she needed to share some with the dog. She made her way to the doorway, offering him the head and tail, which he devoured in a single gulp. "You had the little fish," she reminded him as she backed into the turf hut to finish her meal beside the fire.

"People gone," the old man said. "Only I remain."

She found that she understood him more easily now that she was getting used to his manner of speaking. "Where did they go?" she asked.

The old man gummed his fish, noisily smacking his lips after each swallow. She recognized the sound of the toothless old and waited for him to pause between bites. But he said no more.

Still waiting, she turned the big fish on the fire.

After she had licked her fingers clean, she tried again. "How do you get food?"

"Otter," he replied. "Raise her. You. You are not Keeper of Story. She said...she said..."

Willow blurted, "She? Great Mother?"

When he remained silent, Willow spoke again, certain now of a connection. "If Great Mother came to you, she must have told you I was next."

"Next Keeper not ready." He paused, breathing heavily, then said, "Too late to give back. Too late."

"Give what back?" she asked.

He shook his head. "Our women. Our children. Taken."

"Who?" Willow pressed. "Who took them?"

"People of Singing Seals," he said. He paused again. "You are not Keeper then. Keeper knows Story. Knows at start we are one, one people. Knows how, long ago after Wave, our few journey inland to live. Later, People of Singing Seals come for trees. Our few meet them gladly. They take our children. Then come back, steal again, all girls. Next time we meet them with stones. Many hurt. Now when they come for trees, they dare not tarry. They fear us, fear stones. Never come this way. Only Marrow."

"Marrow," Willow murmured. He must mean Great Mother, whom Willow had never known by any other name. Great Mother, here?

"Go back, you. Tell them too late to return what their fathers' fathers steal. They need not know only this old one remains. Let them fear. Take dog away so otter comes."

"If I send the dog away, I go as well," Willow told him.

The old man nodded, dismissing her.

Willow drew closer to the hot embers. She thought of asking whether she could carry some away with her. Carry them where? Back to the rock shelter, she supposed. She would drag out this last warm moment before going.

She straightened. Only now did she think of her boots left soaked at the edge of the lake. She considered asking him if she could dry off some belongings by his fire before she left, but she could see him darting looks at the dog lying just outside the opening.

She wondered how she could reach some giving impulse in this man. Or maybe she should just remind him that she had brought him the fish. If she was forced to leave with the dog, he would have no use of her net or her prowess.

But now that his belly was full and he had another great fish ready for eating, he seemed to have lost interest in Willow. She would prove herself useful only by removing the dog from his doorway. Then he would probably lie back in the smoky comfort of his hut and wait for the otter to make its way back to him.

She left without another word. The wind had subsided. She could even feel the sun. She and the dog walked back to the lake. Both drank. Then she pulled on the dank sealskin boots and headed uphill to the stone shelter. This time she led the way.

17

After leaving her things in the rock shelter, Willow spent the brief midday digging exposed turf. Before dark she had a heap of uneven peat blocks spread out to dry, but nothing to burn. She thought of raiding the old man's supply. Would he notice a bit of missing tinder? She could replace it with some of the turf she had just exposed to the air. He should be willing to share. He should even invite her to share the space and warmth of his earthen hut.

She would inform him of his obligations to a person without fire. Probably he had lived so long by himself that he had forgotten the ways of people who live together. Hadn't she brought him fish, more fish than they could eat at one sitting?

As she headed down to the turf hut, the dog at her side, she pondered what he had told her about her people and his. What could she believe? Even if once long ago they had all been one, it seemed possible that after the Wave, when the survivors were desperate, a few might have splintered off from the larger group on the coast. But surely she would have heard about stolen children. If the old man had spent his whole life fighting off the People of the Singing Seals, he must be older than...than anyone.

Great Mother had been a small child when the sky turned yellow and the Wave swept almost everyone to their deaths, leaving nothing behind but broken bodies and tools and boats and other unrecognizable scraps of their lives. Maybe this old man had been a child then too.

Willow wondered what it had been like for the few who fled inland, so far from the sea that was their livelihood before the Wave. By the time the valley of trees had become a barrier, something else must have happened.

The old man maintained that after the Wave the People of the Singing Seals did cross that boundary. That was when they carried off young women and girls. It was only afterward that his people concealed themselves to launch attacks whenever the People of the Singing Seals came near. But that wasn't what the uncles and women claimed whenever they spoke of the Others who lurked on the other side of the valley. The Others were a hostile people with deadly aim.

Willow could remember Great Mother silently distancing herself from the uncles' fearful warnings. But Great Mother never did tell the true story behind the threat the Others posed. Since every story belonged to one Story, she was always waiting for Willow to learn each in its place. Only then would Willow be ready to learn the next.

Now when it was too late, she felt like pleading with Great Mother to share this story of the Others. Or did Great Mother want Willow to discover it on her own? When Great Mother left, she must have expected that Willow would venture beyond the valley of trees, just as Great Mother had done in her time.

As Willow neared the turf hut, the dog left to go to the lake for a drink. Willow hesitated. Then, quickly, she strode up to the doorway and stooped to peer inside. "I have come back," she said into the smoky darkness. "For turf," she added when there was no reply.

Something stirred, but the old man didn't speak. She stepped inside, savoring the warmth from the hearth. Slowly the old man emerged from a pile of skins. The otter stretched and eyed her.

"Too late," the old man said.

"I only want enough to stay warm this night," she told him.

"You are sent too late," he said. "All are gone but me."

"No," she tried to explain. "I told you. I am the next Keeper of Story."

He knelt to stir the embers and then placed one more peat slab on the glowing ash. She decided to ask him for a bit of live fire to go with the turf. First she would remind him of the food she had brought to his hearth. And she hadn't yet mentioned the circle of stones.

"Where is that big fish?" she asked.

The old man cast his eyes around the dark enclosure. "Gone," he said. "Otter."

"You fed that whole fish to the otter?" she demanded.

"Otter," he responded.

She was furious. She had fed the dog nothing but the head and tail of the remaining half of her fish. She glared at the otter. The sleek beast returned her look with its bright, dark eyes. Then it slid lazily onto its side and stretched out on the skins.

The old man eyed his beast, his jumbled bedding. He glanced at Willow as if surprised to find her still there. He raised his scrawny arm and pointed at the doorway.

"How am I to know what is true and what is not?" she demanded. "I do not think Great Mother, who has long been Keeper of Story, could come this distance, at least not in recent times."

The old man shrugged. "Not so far."

"It is many days of walking from the valley of trees," Willow retorted.

"Not when straight," he told her.

"Straight…" Willow faltered. The old man seemed to have an answer for everything. "But there is no way to tell straight."

"Stones," the old man said. "Markers."

"The stone circle?" asked Willow.

He shook his head. "Markers like circle already here when few come after Wave. Stones still standing when Marrow finds way. Later, knock down markers lest more People of Singing Seals come. Let People fear, says Marrow. Let them always shun danger."

"She never said," Willow murmured. Even when Great Mother had known she was leaving, even then she had held all this back from Willow. And now she must learn it to become the true Keeper of Story.

She helped herself to small peat clumps and used them to nudge a lighted fragment from the fire. Holding them as close as possible without smothering the live ember, she went outside to the dog. The precious ember glowed as they walked uphill through the dark.

18

Waking in the rock shelter was dismal. The small fire Willow had coaxed alive had died, and no warmth remained in the dim space she had shared with the dog.

He was already outside, staring at the otter slicing through the lake and then crouching over the fish it carried ashore. As far as Willow could see, the otter devoured the entire fish. Then it groomed itself, intent on removing every trace of blood and scales. Clearly it served itself before any other.

So this could be the right time to attend to the old man's needs. Maybe he would come to appreciate Willow through what she provided.

She ducked back inside the shelter, grabbed the net, and headed for the lake. "No," she said in a warning tone as the dog's gaze fastened on the otter. "No," she repeated, a restraining hand on his head.

He seemed to understand, but she could tell that the strain was almost unbearable. It made her think of the strife between the raiding People of the Singing Seals and the Others, the inland survivors who had turned on those who had injured them. Once they had become hunter as well as hunted, the conflict fed on itself. So it was with the dog and the otter, although Willow couldn't be sure which was the hunter and which the hunted. So it was with the old man and all he retained of his people's loss and rage.

She was mindful of this deep distrust as she fished for him and for herself. Each time she netted a big fish, she stopped to dump it flapping into Crab's sack. By the time she splashed out of the water, the otter was nowhere to be seen and the dog was lying tense and glum on the stony bank.

"Good," she said to the dog. "That was good. You have to let this otter go."

He rose slowly and wagged his tail, but she didn't let herself believe that he understood what she had said. Only the tone of approval. Clearly he had liked its sound.

She approached the turf hut cautiously, one hand extended toward the dog to remind him of the strange new rule she had imposed on him. It occurred to her that he might be as unaccustomed to live otters as she was. It must have looked to him like prey. But now that she had seen it devour its own catch, she suspected that if it had to fight for its life or even for food, its killing prowess would be proved.

Willow looked down at the dog, his scarred head and crumpled ear reminders of what he had already endured in the time before she knew him. Someday he would be overcome by a younger and stronger dog or by a beast with sharper teeth and deadly intent. She stopped abruptly to kneel beside him, then threw her arm around his shoulders. He stood quite still, his head bowed, submitting to her embrace. She guessed this was the first time he had been clasped like this. She couldn't tell what it meant to him or even whether he felt anything that resembled her own need of their closeness.

When she left him outside the hut, she gave him one of the fish. She watched for a moment while he nosed it, almost tossing it in the air as if he were enacting the ritual of the kill. Then he looked up at Willow.

"Yours," she told him. "Yes."

Poised over the dead fish, he seemed to be waiting for her to turn away, to make a show of leaving it for him. So she did turn, stooping to enter the hut once again. As she approached the fire, she could hear the dog beginning to feed on the fish.

It took a while for her to realize that the hut was empty. She had to call, in case the smoky dark interior concealed the old man.

She hesitated before stirring the embers. As soon as the fire flared up and then subsided, she placed three fish on it and then went out to find the dog frantically pawing at his mouth and gagging. Quickly she stuck her hand between his jaws, found the offending bone, and yanked it out. He bit down hard as she withdrew her hand, and she cried out in surprise. He cowered, averting his head, then lay abject with saliva drooling from his mouth.

She clutched herself, then examined the bite marks, finding punctures as well as deep scrapes where the dog's teeth had raked the back of her hand. The old man came upon her like this, saw the cowering dog, and swung his stick at him. The dog yelped and leaped away.

"No dog!" the old man declared.

Willow went straight to the dog and offered her hand. After glancing uneasily back at the old man, the dog sniffed her and began to lick the wounds. She settled beside him, then looked up defiantly at the old man. "Yes dog," she told him. "He will not hunt your otter. There is fish inside. For all of us. For dog too," she added, only afterward remembering that the dog had been choking on a bone from a fish he had just consumed. As long as the dog kept on licking, she would remain with him.

After a moment the old man went into his turf hut. At least the otter wasn't there. Yet. Willow decided she would be sure to secure her own portion and another for the dog before the old man squandered it all on his ravenous beast.

19

That day Willow gave the old man her name, and he told her his was Wrack. Knowing only the sea wrack that grows around offshore ledges, she asked him what land wrack looked like. He mulled her question a while before replying. At first she couldn't understand and thought she must have misheard his strange-sounding words.

They were standing outside the hut soaking up the last of the sun's weak warmth. Most of the snow had blown off the undulating heath, but a few white veins remained, marking steeper inclines and taller grasses. She gazed from heath to lake and across to more of the same. Finally she blurted, "But you are inland. You cannot know sea wrack."

He growled his reply: "You cannot be Keeper of Story. You do not know enough."

"I am," she protested. "I was not quite ready when Great Mother went, but I am all they have. All they had," she amended.

"Have yet," he told her. "If Keeper, you."

She shook her head. She didn't tell him that the People of the Singing Seals had turned against Great Mother. They would reject Willow's storytelling too. They had but one use for her, and that was to produce new life. She shivered. If she returned, she would be given to an uncle. She would not return to become prey.

The man stood awhile without speaking. Then suddenly he said, "If you be sent to repair past harm, not enough. Too late. Yet you claim you are not sent. So. If not to begin righting old wrong, why come, you? Are you Boundless?"

Willow gasped. "You know of the Boundless?"

Wrack sent her a look she couldn't fathom. Of course he must wonder how one solitary girl had appeared out of nowhere when none of her people dared cross into his land.

"She told you!" Willow exclaimed. "Great Mother told you!"

"She tells," Wrack replied. "There is echo for me in her telling. Maybe from long ago."

The dog stiffened and uttered a low growl. Willow held out a restraining hand but didn't touch him. Then she caught sight of the otter returning to the turf hut. The lithe beast swerved away, poised for flight.

"Take dog from here," Wrack ordered sharply.

Once again Willow was startled. A moment ago they had been close to exploring a shared story. Now he seemed ready to stone her and the dog to drive them away.

She set off at once without looking back, but she supposed the otter and the old man were quickly reunited. The dog stayed close beside her, no longer driven to lead, to seek, to arrive with her at a destination. They had nowhere to go but back to the rock shelter.

She used the rest of the brief daylight to dig up peat and stack it to dry. The dog lazed beside her, his eyes half shut, his great muscled body relaxed.

They couldn't stay here for long. The old man wanted them gone. He preferred solitude to their presence. She would let him know that they would be on their way just as soon as he told her everything he could remember about Great Mother.

Later, when she and the dog were lying close for warmth, she wondered what the old man knew about the Boundless. An echo, Wrack had said. An echo from before the Wave?

After the Wave, after the Others became separated from

their people, what else was lost to them? Wrack had asked Willow if she was Boundless. Did he fail to grasp that only the Boundless live through time? Even Great Mother had been prepared to die.

Maybe he was so old that his thinking was becoming as feeble as his body. Except that Wrack's thin and bent body wasn't really wasted. His scrawny arms didn't prevent him from defending his otter with hard and well-aimed stones.

Sometime during the night, howling dogs woke her. She listened to their mingled voices and guessed they must be the three she had encountered. When the pack at home went night hunting and their howls floated back to the hut cluster, their sound was fuller, the calls and responses drawn in waves of wild song. These fewer howls soon subsided. A solitary yelp set them off once more, but only briefly. She imagined that one had become separated from the other two. Satisfied with what her mind depicted, she was sinking back into sleep when the dogs could be heard again, more distant now.

The dog beside her lifted his head and uttered a soft moan. The moan opened into a muted howl and then faded. Heaving a sigh, he settled down once more.

For one moment Willow was transfixed. Once in a while a pack dog at home would respond like that to the seals when they sang from their offshore ledges. The haunting sound always filled her with wonder and sadness. Hearing it now so far from home, she could feel the pack ties. Even this dog who had become Thorn's companion and then hers seemed to long for some other connection. Still, it puzzled her that even when the pack dogs had each other, the singing seals could reach across the shallows to at least one of them.

Now, far from home, this dog's own song was finished almost as soon as it had begun. He stretched and turned, his back against hers, their warmth mingling.

20

Willow lurched awake. The dog stood in the shelter opening, not moving. It took a moment for her to realize they weren't alone. In the early light of day the figure that seemed more shadow than substance hovered just outside. It was strange that while the dog seemed to be blocking the entrance, he wasn't growling.

She rose and stepped toward him. The figure was indeed a man. The old man, stopped now but neither cowering nor turning to flee the dog he knew to be menacing.

"What?" she asked as she went to stand beside the dog.

"Tell Boundless story, you. Then I know."

"Now?" she asked. "I can come to your hut in a while and—"

"Now," he said, nodding toward the shelter.

His urgent tone was baffling. She backed inside, but the dog remained where he was, blocking Wrack's entry. "Wait," she said to the old man. She walked outside. The dog went with her. "You go in," she told Wrack. "Then I will come."

The old man entered while she and the dog relieved themselves. Then as they approached the shelter together, she tried with an extended hand to restrain the dog. But either he didn't understand or he chose to ignore her. So let this old man accept the dog, she decided. He had come seeking her story here in her place.

Wrack was squatting beside the cold ashes. He eyed the dog but didn't back away. The dog sank down onto the stone floor. Willow could see that man and dog were still wary, though maybe growing used to each other.

Wrack, unaccustomed to the rock shelter, which was so much colder than his turf hut, seemed drawn to the makeshift hearth even though it yielded no heat at all. He appeared to Willow like one near death.

She would hurry through the story of the Boundless so that Wrack could return to his own warm place while he still had the strength to walk there. She didn't think she needed to tell the entire story in the exact words Great Mother had taught her, so she skipped at once to the crucial part where Star the Boundless went to sea with his companions and wandered beyond the horizon until they arrived at the Last Island.

Wrack scowled, shook his head, and raised one hand. "That is not whole of it," he complained.

"I hasten the telling so that you may return to the comfort of your fire," she told him.

"Then I cannot know if you be Keeper. Tell whole, you."

So that was why he demanded the story. Not to recall what he might have lost, but to confirm that she could recite every word of it, every rise and fall of voice that is passed through time from Keeper to Keeper.

She shut her eyes. The words rose up from deep within and flowed in perfect cadence. Her telling became one with Great Mother's. Her eyes stayed closed as the story emptied out of her, all of it, from Star and his companions setting out upon the sea to their arrival and landfall on the Last Island, where they are made welcome, where they are warned they can never return to their homeland, for if they do, they will crumble to dust. They remain on the Last Island for countless lifetimes, thriving and content, until one of Star's companions pines for his home and his former life.

"So Star and his men set off once more," Willow intoned. "They wander long upon the pathless sea in search of home. Finally they see a familiar shoreline and head for it. There, folk gather on the beach to greet them."

Willow could feel herself sway to the rhythm of these words, her voice lifting and sinking with the story's lilt. "Yet no one on shore can recognize Star or his men. When he tells them his name, the homeland folk can only say that Star the Boundless is in their ancient stories."

Willow drew a long breath before concluding. "When Star turns his boat away from the homeland, the man who yearned to return leaps from the vessel and splashes ashore. The instant he stumbles onto the beach, he vanishes, and where he stood there is only a small mound of ashes, which the next wave carries off.

"Then Star's boat glides away toward the setting sun and is seen no more."

Willow was inside the story that had been inside her. For a while she remained still and silent. When finally she was restored to her surroundings, the first thing that she heard was the old man's rough breathing, then the dog licking a paw, and after that some bird that braved the cold time to call from the sky. Willow shivered. She opened her eyes.

Wrack still squatted, his bony knees jutting out like featherless wings. Without looking directly at her, he said, "So. You be Keeper. Now I tell what you may seek to know. She comes, Marrow, old Keeper of Story. Last time comes from sea. Like man who longs for homeland. Only Marrow does not crumble to ashes."

Trying to absorb what he was saying, Willow fixed him with a look. But he wouldn't meet her eyes. Was he saying that Great Mother had come on a boat? But that couldn't be, unless he meant a land boat.

"There is no sea here," Willow blurted. "There is only land, forbidden land, on this side of the valley of trees. The sea is on the other side of the valley, on the far side of the land I come from."

Wrack scowled. "Then you are not quite Keeper, for you are at same time too sure and too ignorant. But since you may yet be next Keeper, although unready, I will tell you where to find sea—and more."

Thoroughly bewildered, Willow didn't know whether to dismiss what he promised or pay strict attention to whatever he told her, no matter how misleading. She might need to pick through his telling in search of some hidden speck of truth.

Wrack struggled to his feet, his limbs creaking with the strain. "First refresh, you. Then come to my hut."

He didn't offer to share the fish she had brought him or the fire that must still lie glowing beneath a bank of ash on his hearth. She was tempted to decline his ungenerous invitation, but curiosity held her in check. For the first time since she had arrived at this place she was beginning to believe that he really might know more than he had been willing to say so far. So she nodded, stepping back to give him space, and then watched him shamble to the opening and leave.

21

Willow didn't hurry. The old man wasn't going anywhere far, and she was too hungry and cold to postpone attending to her needs.

But as she prepared to step into the lake, the dog appeared over the brow of the turf-exposed hill. He trotted stiffly, his head held at an awkward angle so that the hare clenched between his jaws didn't drag on the ground. Spared the cold immersion, Willow ran to meet him.

The hare was large enough for all of them. As soon as the dog yielded it up to her, she reached for the fire stone in her pouch and then stuffed the net back inside it. But then she thought better of skinning the hare on the lakeshore. No need to draw the wild dogs to the scent. So she carried the hare and fire stone and pouch up to the turf hut.

Without looking inside, she called to Wrack, "Prepare a fire. The dog brought us hare." She thought for a moment and added, "To share with him." Then she knelt on the beaten earth at the side of the doorway and spread the carcass before her. The first precise cuts with the fire stone opened the flawless white pelt to reveal the unmarred flesh. Determined not to damage either skin or meat, she managed with the sharp-edged stone and her own breath to separate the two and slip the one from the other. Proudly she carried them through the doorway.

The old man blinked at her, blinked at the hare, as if unsure of what he saw. As soon as she moved away from the glare behind her, he opened his eyes wider and then nodded his approval. Now she had to adjust her sight to the gloom inside. There were flames, and there was ash spread to the side of the hearth. She had no idea why he had removed ashes from the fire. What mattered at this moment was cooking the meat. She reached for stones to prop up the carcass, and Wrack didn't interfere.

For a while she was so occupied with managing the coming meal that she forgot the reason for her being here. It wasn't until the sputtering meat juices nearly extinguished the fire that Wrack took charge. First he produced a concave stone to catch the drippings. Then he brushed the cold ashes still farther from the fire. "It is time to sit. And listen," he told her.

But he had fed on fish already, and she was hungry. So she stood up to him. "The dog and I must eat," she said. She glanced around, making sure that the otter was nowhere inside.

Wrack prodded the scorched and steaming meat, then tipped it off the fire.

Poised to snatch what she and the dog required, Willow watched his every move. But of course the meat was too hot to touch. The aroma wafted around them, luring the dog partway inside.

When she could bear the wait no longer, she seized a hindquarter and tore it off. Deliberately she rose and brought it to the dog, who took it from her hand and backed away from the opening. Then she wrenched off a shoulder and foreleg. She held this out to Wrack and waited, the offering suspended above the smoking hearth. But he didn't respond. Well, she thought, there was plenty more when he was ready for it.

Like the dog, like the old man, she backed away a little before beginning to eat.

She supposed she sounded like a beast with its prey as

she gnawed and chewed and swallowed. Juices ran down her chin and inside her wrists and arms. It didn't matter, since the lake could remove the stain and the smell so that no wild dogs would catch the scent of her. But when she rose to go to the water, Wrack gestured to her to stop.

"First hear what I have to tell," he said.

"I will come back," she replied.

"Hear me first, you," he insisted, already crawling to the heap of ashes he had swept away from the hearth. He flattened and smoothed them. "Sea wrack," he reminded her.

Sea wrack, she thought dismissively. This witless old man was about to inform her that it could be found this far from the sea.

Already Wrack was marking the ashes, first a great but sloppy egg shape, then shadow shapes inside and out of it. Next he drew two lines side by side across the middle of the egg shape. "Valley," he said. Then he made a small circle between the two lines. "Trees here," he told her. Pointing to the outside of one end of the egg, he added, "Your land and sea. Marrow tells me of your living place. Tells of sheep and seals and sometimes huge whales, and sometimes great trees, far greater than those your people take from valley for tree boats. Great trees floating from somewhere distant. She does not know where they grow. All this I believe."

Willow nodded. It was the longest speech she had heard from Wrack, and it didn't sound at all like foolish rambling. He wanted to show her that the valley was other than she had thought. It was a rift that cut across the land. The small circle, the valley of trees, was just a part of the valley. "So what do you mark here?" she asked, pointing to the shadow shape at the far end of the section he called the valley of trees.

"Land edge not round and smooth like egg. It is toothed." He made part of the outline jagged. "Still," he explained, sweeping his hand over the outline, "this is shape of land." He bent over the ashes and drew short, broken lines just past the area he designated as her home place. "Waves. Sea," he said, shifting to reach across to the opposite end of the egg shape. Again he made those short wavelike marks. He scooped up a bit of ash into a pile. "Sea cliffs," he said. "Birds."

"But," she blurted, "all is land on this side of the valley."

"Much land, yes. Then sea. Sea wrack, too," he added. "Old Keeper of Story comes this last time from sea. Comes to die, she says. Her Last Island. Only she does not vanish, does not become ashes. She rests on shore. Takes no food or drink, no matter how I would feed her, I and boy with bad leg."

"Thorn!" Willow blurted. "He was here?"

Wrack nodded.

"Where are they now?" she pleaded.

"Gone. Before she dies she tells again of Star the Boundless. She is not Boundless, she says. Yet each Keeper of Story lives through time, she says, through next Keeper, next telling of Story. Then she sleeps, Marrow. Does not wake. Boy, Thorn, covers her with tangle weed. Together we place her where waves cut through cliff. There it be dry and safe. We cover her with many stones. That is all we can do. Marrow."

Willow had known that when Great Mother left for the last time, she was preparing to die. Still, it was a while before she could finally ask, "What about Thorn?"

Wrack shrugged. "Cannot climb cliff, Thorn. Sets off again in same strange craft. Craft has wing made from bird wings."

Willow nodded. She knew all about that winged boat.

"But when? When were they here?" Thorn might have sailed along the coast to find an easier landfall.

"When dark comes to hunt down days."

"Not so long ago," Willow murmured to herself. Where was Thorn now?

After a while she said bleakly, "I never knew enough. I never knew there was another sea beyond the land."

"Or another land beyond the sea," Wrack said. "Maybe Last Island for more than Marrow."

Willow fell silent. Nothing she had been taught made sense right now. She might still seek stories about her people, stories of and for them. But when this old man died, there would be no one left to tell them to. That was what it would be like to remain here alone. After her there would be no next Keeper to gather up the stories and fit them together anew. There would be no one left to keep the Story alive.

22

Willow intended to stay one more night in the rock shelter, but when it snowed again on the following day, she put off leaving. Meanwhile she sorted peat slabs for burning and smoked more fish on her fire. She tried to keep the dog from the turf hut so that the otter could freely come and go. Once she saw the beast cavorting in the snow on its return from a hunt. It stretched and rolled, leaped and plunged, coiling upon itself only to spring once more, black against the glistening white. She couldn't take her eyes off it.

The dog needed no restraining now. When he and the otter came even slightly close to each other, he turned away as if he couldn't bear the otter's vibrant display.

Willow asked Wrack to show her how to find the sea and the shore where Thorn landed and Great Mother was buried.

Standing outside his hut, he pointed toward the rising sun and then away. He marked the direction in ashes and again on the snow. "First see more rock, you. Land rises to cliff. Maybe hear those seabirds that stay through dark time."

She wondered which birds these were. At home most birds flew away when the days grew short. Then they returned before nesting, filling the sky with clamorous cries.

"You may hear other sea sounds as well," Wrack told her.

Thinking of bird eggs and the crabs and clams that could always be found in the sand, she asked, "Why do you live so far from the sea? And where are other huts?"

"When my people see how Wave takes everything, they go far from sea. They build turf huts. Only mine remains. After people die, huts become fuel to burn."

Willow couldn't imagine living away from the sea and its creatures. "You have no sheep, then," she said, glancing at the deerskin draped around his body.

Wrack said, "We take some that wander out of valley where they sometimes go to bear young. But dogs soon kill them."

"Our sheep can escape to the ledges. That is where they feed. On the seaweed."

"On this side of valley much is different," he said.

Different, yes, she thought. What would it be like to remain here with one aging dog? She supposed she must return home. At least she would see Crab. Thinking of him reminded her of the lengthening days to come and how they always climbed the sea stack together, each of them daring the other to raid higher nests, while frantic birds dove at them from above. Even when she and Crab looked out for each other, each was always striving to return with the most eggs, still vying with the other as they showed off their bloodied heads and arms.

For a brief moment Willow was able to forget that her father and the uncles would never again allow her to climb the sea stack with Crab. Then she faced what she knew, that when she went home, all child deeds and daring challenges would be stopped. Her voice, the one belonging to the Keeper of Story, would be silenced as well.

Before she could decide whether to stay or go, she needed to find the place where Great Mother was buried inside the base of a cliff. She might add more stones to protect her. After that she would consider searching along the coast for any sign that Thorn had landed again. If he had, then he would surely need help through the cold time.

She wondered whether the dog would be able to tell if Thorn was near. It troubled her that he showed no eagerness to set forth again. His only sign of restlessness came at night when the wild dogs howled—he would stir and sometimes whine. Then his tension would subside and he would sleep.

The snow blew off the hill first. When it disappeared from the surrounding heath, Willow made a few attempts to look for the coast. Unburdened by her pouch and sack, she made swift and hopeful starts. But she could only go so far before she had to turn back, unwilling to spend a night in the open. The turning point usually came after she had climbed one final hill, certain that from there she would glimpse a cliff and maybe even the sea itself. But always the expanse of moorland stretched away, unbroken, except when she caught sight of distant deer.

"How far is it?" she asked Wrack as she scraped and kneaded the inside of the hare pelt. "Maybe you forgot the way."

"I do not forget. I am there when strange craft comes. I help boy with shriveled leg. We tend Marrow, who is Keeper of Story."

"How did you walk that far?" she demanded, her voice strident as she pummeled the pelt.

"Slowly. Easily. More than one day and one night and another day," he told her.

"Did no beasts attack you after dark?" she asked.

He shrugged. "I carry fire. I am not afraid."

Willow considered what he said. She too might carry live

embers. Anyway, before she could decide how and where she was to live, she would find Great Mother's burial place to see for herself that the Keeper of Story slept her long sleep undisturbed. A day and a night and a day. That wasn't nearly as long as Willow's wandering before she arrived at this place. She would leave the pelt where the old man could keep track of it. She would be back to claim it and to finish the softening, and then she would ask him to show her the straight way to the valley of trees.

Back in the rock shelter she placed a stone slab on her pouch and packed Crab's sack with the fire stone, smoked fish, and the sheepskin cover. She would wait until she was about to leave before wrapping embers. She had forgotten to ask Wrack whether there was water along the way. Still, even if he had said there was, she couldn't be certain that she would find his exact path. She was prepared now, ready to set forth at first light. This time she would keep going.

23

The early morning sky seemed to glower over the heath, but the wind had subsided. A fine day, thought Willow, once again full of vigor and hope. Still, she halted often to check her direction, the dim sunlight ahead at first, then later at her shoulder when she turned, the shoulder that usually bore Crab's sack. The muted light came and went, deceptive behind the low gray cloud.

When the hills grew steeper, she began to look for outcrops of rock. Stopping on a summit to cast her eyes over the surrounding land, her gaze fell on a swath of brighter green. She started downhill. Now far below her she could see shrub willow and hazel and the glint of a bog pool in the lowland.

The slender hazel branches made Willow think of Hazel's frantic flailing and how it had upset the boat. Willow cringed as she recalled her own rage and her callous treatment of the weaker girl. It seemed now as if Hazel's weakness had always been a kind of goad. Never again, Willow promised herself. This journey had changed her. She would banish anger when she returned home. If she returned.

She was approaching the green lowland and thinking of home when the ground shuddered beneath her. She stopped so that her feet could hear what had not yet reached her ears. The dog stood rigid, listening and looking. Then he bounded away.

Willow stared after him. Deer. They came pounding from the bog scrub, three dogs in pursuit. Willow watched as the dogs pressed the deer and the deer sought firmer turf. She guessed that the dogs had surprised the deer as they browsed. Once they gained solid ground, they were likely to escape.

But another dog charged forward to meet the small herd, which panicked and split at this confrontation. Before Willow could even see the crumpled ear, she recognized the dog and knew that he had responded as a pack beast.

One deer at the rear of the herd hesitated between the two fleeing groups. The dog hurled himself at her throat. After a few more paces, she staggered and fell. By then the wild dogs were upon her.

The first moments after the kill told Willow all she needed to know about how the dog might fare if he remained with this small pack. At first as all the dogs tore at the carcass, Willow couldn't even tell which was which. Vapor rose from their feeding ground like steam rising from a cauldron.

But as soon as Thorn's dog backed away to eat what he had dragged from the carcass, the other dogs became aware of him. When he tried to return, there was a challenge, a warning snarl. He stayed back until the others returned to their feeding. Then he darted in to snatch another mouthful. The leader of the wild dogs snapped at him, but that was all. Willow supposed that if Thorn's dog joined this small pack, he might have to keep his distance for a while, but he would get a share of the kill.

She continued on down the hill to the bog pool, where she knelt to drink. There were deer droppings around the willow and hazel and other low-lying shrubs. She guessed that the old man or his people must have come with throwing stones to ambush deer that browsed here. Could she learn to hunt that way? Could she survive here as Wrack had done on his own?

The dog came to wallow in the pool and lap the brown water. He had a small gash under his eye, one more wound to leave its scar. While he bathed and drank, she ate some smoked fish. It occurred to her that if she had brought the hare pelt along, she could have left it here to soak in the peaty water to hasten the curing.

After the dog came out, slathered with mud, he shook and then looked for a patch of sedge to roll in. Willow saw with a pang how content he was, not only because he had eaten well but because of his encounter with his kind.

He finished rolling, shook off debris, and set about marking every nearby shrub. She could tell he meant to return to this place.

24

The heath seemed endless. Willow and the dog kept going until the brief daylight began to recede. Since there was no apparent shelter, Willow looked for a hollow where they could spend the long night. Knowing how the wind tended to rise before the sun set, she settled for a spot on the far side of one of the steeper hills, a mere incline below the crest. Here there might be some protection from gusts sweeping over the open land.

The ember, packed too tight, had gone cold. Willow refused to be discouraged. They were well on their way, the dog had eaten his fill, and there was a sheepskin to share. She grabbed a few mouthfuls of fish, let the dog lick her fingers, and settled down on the cold ground, where she promptly fell asleep.

She woke once when the dog sat up. She listened but heard nothing. Maybe some silent night hunter had struck its prey nearby. The dog's nose twitched. After a moment he tried to dig where he had lain, gave up, and curled beside Willow once more.

By morning she was hungry. The remaining fish tempted her, but she had to think of the return journey when there might be greater need.

There was wind now, but from a different direction. If the setting sun had been behind her, the wind should be at her back. It wasn't, though. It was a headwind with such a stinging lash that her face burned. Was she going the wrong way? She had to keep assuring herself that the rising sun was still before her and off that same shoulder.

Fighting the wind, her head bowed, she didn't realize until the land leveled off that she had been climbing for a long while. Here on this plateau fierce gusts slammed her so hard that she staggered. The dog struggled too, his muzzle low, his good ear whipped back.

And then she saw swirling mist rising up from some unimaginable depth. Instinctively she crouched, feeling her way close to the ground until the ground itself ended. She was at the edge of a great headland, its shelving cliffs shrouded in sea smoke. Far below her, waves seethed and crashed on long, flat rocks sloping shoreward. Through the mist she caught only glimpses of this violent meeting of sea and land.

Her first thought was of Thorn. If he had approached along this shoreline, wouldn't the wind-driven waves have pounded his craft to bits? Yet Wrack claimed that Thorn had brought Great Mother to die near this place. So maybe the flaying wind wasn't constant. Maybe this sea could change from one day to the next like the sea at home.

Battered and overwhelmed, she backed away from the cliff edge. She needed respite from the wind, but she didn't know where to go. At least she had found the sea. Wrack had not misled her.

As she retreated, the thought came to her that here too the wind blew in from the sea. This was baffling. Maybe it wasn't the setting sun at home or the rising sun here that determined the wind's direction. Maybe the sea itself possessed the wind and thrust it landward.

With no possible shelter in sight, Willow crawled back to the cliff and began to search for a way down to the shore. Ahead where the coastline turned she glimpsed a deep chasm and then another farther along. In one such place Great Mother lay buried. Peering down through sea smoke at black rocks streaked with white bird droppings, Willow saw no living thing. Still, she caught glimpses of nesting sites along the cliff face.

The dog was surprisingly fearful and shrank from the edge as he crawled after her. When she came to a break in the turf, she stretched out on her stomach to gaze down. The dog whimpered. She wanted him to stay while she looked for a way from here. She knew how the face of a cliff can crumble underfoot, how stone and earth give way, how root and rock slide out from beneath a climber. She didn't want to risk his safety while she tried out one place after another.

As soon as she swiveled and let her feet down, she lost her nerve. It was almost as though the dog's fear had undercut her prowess. She dangled briefly before hauling herself back up.

At the next break in the cliff edge, she was able to see more clearly. A short way down, a shallow ledge followed the contour of the cliff face. The turf shelving looked worn with use. She couldn't imagine what beast would clamber up and down here, but if it had been used, it must have sustained some weight. Carefully lowering herself and swinging her legs until her feet touched the narrow shelf, she paused to scope out her next step.

The wind helped, pressing her against the cliff. She located another landing spot and slowly edged toward it. The dog whimpered and then slid, forefeet first, to reach her. After that, bit by bit, they made their way, more often sideways than straight down, until finally they stood together on a great slab of rock.

Just below them waves crashed, spray and foam rimming

the great slab of rock where they stood. Willow's legs were trembling, her fingers raw, and every muscle ached. But she was elated. They had arrived.

Arrived where?

First they needed to get out of the wind and catch their breath. She looked each way, saw nothing likely, and began to clamber over an immense boulder that blocked her view of the coastline ahead. The dog scrambled seaward to skirt the boulder. She thought the waves would seize him, but he reappeared as she slid to the other side. He was drenched and his bloodshot eyes looked crazed, but he was still with her.

Their struggle was rewarded, for there beyond the boulder a great cut opened into the cliff. It even had a sandy bottom with shell drift. Willow heaved herself over the shells and sank down.

"We are here," she declared in triumph. Never mind that here was nowhere and that they would have to find their way back up. The sand felt like home. The shells smelled like home. She leaned back against rough upright stone and drew a deep breath. The dog flopped over on his side and closed his streaming eyes.

25

Willow was tempted to stay for a while. They were both exhausted, and they were out of the wind as long as they clung to the wall of this narrow inlet. But she didn't know whether the sea was rising, and she could tell from the shell drift that waves might reach this far. Besides, she had no idea how long it would take to find Great Mother's burial place and then find a way up and back from there.

Before setting out again, she paused to dig into the sand. Almost at once small jets of water spurted up, telltale signs of clams. She dug harder, the dog now up and at her side to extend and enlarge the hollow. The clams revealed were huge. Greedily she piled them up until she realized she had more than she could eat and carry.

She used the sharp edge of Thorn's fire stone to pry open the first clam. She ripped it from its shell and swallowed too fast, nearly choking on it. Still, she couldn't stop from opening another and then another. After she had eaten her fill, she threw a few to the dog. He sniffed cautiously and then snapped them up, but she could tell he wasn't really hungry.

She packed clams in with her smoked fish, and topped off the load with some of the best shells. There was no telling when she might find a use for them. It occurred to her that she would be carrying a heavy weight that could affect her balance. Still, she wouldn't unload those precious clams to lighten her pack. She was sure she could go almost anywhere sustained on such perfect food.

When she set out again, she glanced back. She wanted to be certain that she would recognize the place where they had descended. The boulder helped. Since they might encounter others, she fixed it in her mind, its size and shape and position.

The going was slow, the footing treacherous. When coastal debris blocked them and forced them into the sea, Willow feared for the dog. She tried to time their wading with receding waves, but sometimes both she and the dog got slapped and dragged before they could regain solid rock.

They came to another cut similar to their first resting place, but there was no sign of a burial, so they kept on. At the next possible spot, they did stop to rest and to drink the fresh water that seeped down inside. Willow used a clamshell to catch drips for the dog.

On they went, the coastal rock spreading and flattening before them and exposing patches of sand draped with tangle weed. Crabs scuttled out of their path, gulls and fulmars swooping down to seize them. Soon the fulmars were attacking Willow and the dog too. Willow had to walk along with arms flailing while the dog leaped up to snap at the plummeting birds.

At least they were on solid footing now. Ahead of them the coastline curved and flattened. The sea seemed to have scooped out a great portion of the coast, leaving behind this broad, sandy cove. All she could see at its far flank was more land. Maybe this was where the sea ended. But Wrack had drawn a great egg-shaped land surrounded by water.

Walking along as she pondered her confusion, she gazed down at the littered sand. Then she looked up and found that what she saw ahead was altered. Now that she was midway across the expanse of beach and still facing the farther tip of the cove, she could glimpse water beyond it. She ran forward a few paces to be sure. Ahead of her the cove ended in an elongated sand spit. The sea was there. It was everywhere. It was boundless.

She stopped short because the dog had halted, his muzzle pointing inland at another cut in the cliff. Willow turned to it. She couldn't detect what the dog smelled, but she knew at once that here was Great Mother's burial place. The shell drift was breached, the sand dug away. And there, way inside, were slabs of stone, one upon another, too neatly stacked to have been deposited by waves.

The dog was intensely curious about the heaped-up stone. Willow only wanted to assure herself that nothing would invade the piled rock and trouble Great Mother's long sleep through time. Great Mother had reached her Last Island. Maybe Great Mother believed that this Last was also the First, her birthplace.

The stones had been selected and laid with such care that Willow could almost feel Thorn's hand on them. Great Mother slept enclosed in a fitting mound.

Willow couldn't leave without adding a stone to the pile. She searched the beach until she came across one in the shape of an egg. It would stand for this island.

She had to shift a few of the flatter stones to place hers at the summit. That was when she caught sight of markings incised on what had been the top slab. There was a shadow shape of the craft that Thorn had made and that had carried Great Mother here. Willow traced the deep lines with her fingertips. "Thorn," she whispered. "Great Mother."

Out on the open beach, she peered up at the cliff to

determine where the old man might have turned to begin his climb. There were several likely pathways. She changed the pack to her other shoulder and headed for the nearest starting place.

26

Back on the turf, she gazed inland at perfect sameness. Not one distinguishing feature appeared, no rocky outcrop or steep hillock or even clumps of reed. Since it was impossible to guess how far she had strayed on her approach to the sea, it would be hopeless to head inland from here. If she meant to return to the rock shelter and turf hut, she would have to follow the coastline until she came to the precipice where she and the dog had so recklessly descended the cliff.

The light was already fading, but the wind had abated, so she was able to keep close to the edge. The sea mist had cleared, too. Mighty waves still tumbled landward, but their turbulence had changed to measured swells. Willow marveled at the transformation. She could live near this coast. She really could.

She wondered whether Thorn had this same thought. But he would have realized that with only one usable leg he couldn't survive here on his own. His only other choice was to return to sea. Willow shuddered, thinking of him alone in his craft in waves as fierce as those just past. Still, he had known the sea when he set out. He had chosen his escape from the People of the Singing Seals, as Willow, despite less knowledge of the sea, had chosen hers. It came to her now as she walked along that Thorn, whether Boundless or not, would always choose the sea.

As the land rose, Willow kept glancing down at the rocky shore. She was afraid of missing what she hoped to recognize. But everything looked so different from this height, especially now that the relentless dark had begun to close around her.

Eventually she had to give in to early night. Moving back from the edge of the cliff, she tried to settle down. But the dog was restless. She guessed that he smelled or heard deer. Or else other dogs.

Huddling alone under the sheepskin, she breathed in traces of heather and thrift. A wave of longing broke over her. At home, plants like those, rooted on the coastal margin, tended to remain supple and fragrant even when they were dormant through the cold time. Here, too, everything that grew close to the cliff retained some moist scent of greening. Its sweetness blended with the salt tang of the sea.

She wondered what Crab was doing. She thought of Hazel and imagined her recovered. With Two Trunk Tree? But Hazel belonged with Thistle, not with an uncle. And Willow? Without Great Mother, without Thorn, where did Willow belong?

She imagined telling Crab what she had learned about the Others. She would begin with long ago when they had all been one people until separated, first by the killing Wave and afterward by raids and revenge. Still, he might reject her story. Or maybe not. If Crab would dare to cross from the valley of trees, he would be able to confirm what she told him, and then he might even choose to stay with her on this forbidden land.

The dog came and pawed at the sheepskin. She raised it so that he could creep in beside her. For a moment he brought the night cold. Then his body warmth closed around them both.

She knew now that she would return home. She had to. Already there were signs that the dog was drifting away from her. There would be other encounters with the small pack.

Even if she could count on him through this cold journey, a time would come when he would be drawn to the wild dogs. Knowing this filled her with grief. Yet she could do no more for him than let him go.

When his muted whine woke her, she stroked his muscled shoulder. Comforted, he quieted. That was when she heard distant howls.

"Soon," she whispered close to his crumpled ear. "Soon."

Yet when they arose in the morning, he behaved as usual, staying near and eagerly gobbling his share of clams. The day was bright but cold, the wind rising. Now that she had lightened her load, she set herself a swift pace, the dog trotting beside her.

When at last she caught sight of the boulder, she doubted what she saw. The sea had receded, and the great slabs of rock, now dry, bore a reddish tinge. Above them the boulder stood out, a sandy gray. But how small it appeared. Probably that was because she was looking down from such a height, everything at the bottom distorted.

All she wanted was to gain her bearings and leave this part of the coast behind. Still, now that she was nearing her arrival point, she found herself drawn to the break in the turf that had invited her to that perilous descent. Leaning over the edge to scan the steep and jagged cliff wall, she saw in the clear morning light just how treacherous were those footholds, most of them undercut, mere shelves protruding without support.

Aghast at what she had attempted and what she had risked, she turned away from the cliff and the sea below. Maybe she would be able to retrace her path now that the wind was at her back.

27

She would have missed the bog pool if the dog hadn't veered off the wind to reach it. Once again she had misjudged the way. Even this strong and steady wind could be misleading.

Relieved to have arrived at a place she knew, she drank and washed and then foraged among the greener bushes for stems to chew. Most of them were bitter. Some made her mouth pucker. She took time to strip a slender hazel branch that was still shiny and supple.

At last she caught sight of a clump of nettles. Emptying her sack and turning it inside out, she wrapped her hand in it so that she could pick the leaves without being stung. Then she stuffed them in her sack. If she reached the turf hut before dark, she would look for a stone pot and make nettle broth. That could be a rare gift for Wrack.

She wondered how he would feel when she left him. Now that she had decided to go, it seemed important that she do so freely. That would mean... What did it mean? In the end she would be no different from Hazel. Still, if that was what she chose over a solitary life here, maybe she would feel less like prey.

This was what she told herself. But she found it hard to hold firm to her resolve. Once she and the dog resumed their journey, worry stalked her footsteps. Even though she tried to concentrate on reaching her destination, all through the day a storm of doubt battered her and slowed her progress.

When the land on the horizon rose to reveal something

that could be exposed rock, her heart lifted. Surely she was close. But night crept from behind as if borne on the wind. The outcrop that had loomed ahead merged with the spreading cover of dark.

Then the dog surged ahead of her. She was sure that if she could keep up with him, he would lead her to Wrack's hut or the lake or the rock shelter. So she ran. It crossed her mind that the dog might be heading for the other dogs, but she kept on running.

All at once she heard the dog splash into the lake. She would follow him after she had the stone pot so that she could carry water back to the fire. Panting, she dropped her sack at the entrance to the turf hut and walked into smoke.

Wrack appeared as a blur. She glanced around until she was able to spot the otter as well. After the clarity of the day, the closeness and thickness of the air inside this hut turned her empty stomach. "I must have the cooking pot," she told him. "I brought nettles."

She thought he nodded, but she couldn't be sure. Groping at solid objects ringing the hearth, her fingers closed over the rim of the stone pot. Back outside, she breathed deeply, pulled her net from the sack, and felt her way to the lake. She fished blindly, the tug on her hand informing her when she had netted something big enough to keep. She threw two fish out on the bank for the dog, netted two more, and then stumbled over the pot in her frantic need to find it in the dark and fill it for broth.

Wrack had done nothing to prepare the fire for cooking. Maybe he hadn't understood her. Maybe he had eaten his fill and wanted to sleep. Maybe he was dying.

She wasn't sure how to fend off the otter, which showed a

keen interest in the fish. Wrack made no move to help. If only she could bring in the dog to guard her meal.

Her rush of words did seem to deter the beast. So she chattered while she stuffed one fish on top of the nettles to cook with them. There was still room for another fish on the fire next to the pot. On her side, away from the otter. Meanwhile she told Wrack that she had found the old Keeper's burial and that she had added a stone. She didn't mention the deer hunt, but she did think to ask him not to hurt her dog if he stayed after she went home.

"So you leave," Wrack said when she paused to draw a breath.

"Yes," she replied.

"By time your first child born, I am gone," he told her.

"Do you want to come with me?" she asked.

He snorted. "To hasten my dying?"

"They wouldn't harm one old man," she asserted. But of course there was no telling. The only person she could count on was Crab. He would help Wrack as he had helped Thorn. "There is a boy," she began haltingly. "Two of them. Like me. One at least."

For a while Wrack remained silent. Then he nodded. "So bring them. Bring him. Bring who would come to this side of valley."

She leaned over the steam rising from the open pot. There was a hollow in her stomach, and she didn't think there could ever be enough broth to fill it. Finally she spoke. "The boys would go hungry without sheep. They have little skill with stones. They do not bring down prey as you do." But Wrack's words had already lodged in her thoughts. *Bring who would come.* She might ignore them for a while, but she knew they would remain.

"Boys can learn. There are fish. You find heavy bird with small wings. Bird does not fly. Easy kill. Dogs prefer hare and deer."

She looked around for something to wrap around the pot so that she could lift it from the fire. The hare pelt would work, but it wasn't where she'd left it. She had to haul out her sheepskin again. Then the broth was too hot. She nudged the other fish away from the hearth.

Delayed food was an agony. So was Wrack's notion of bringing here who would come. That thought admitted hope, which, like hunger, was all-consuming. She needed to think. She needed to eat.

20

The next day she rested, fished, and brought drying turf inside the rock shelter. She told Wrack where he could find it. He nodded. She said, "Now tell me what you have done with the hare skin."

"Otter," he said, indicating the beast stretched full-length in the feeble sunshine.

"Otter!" Willow blurted. "Could you not stop that creature from taking it?"

Wrack sent her a look. "Otter gives up what she chooses, nothing more."

Willow glared at the beast, now nearly doubled over, grooming its fine belly fur.

Wrack said, "When I am dead, she will live on. Do her no harm."

"I will be gone too," Willow replied bleakly. She didn't mention the dog again. She still couldn't tell whether he would leave with her or stay.

"Marrow says in time you make strong babies."

"Not yet," Willow retorted. "I am not ready." Then she added, "As I was not ready to be Keeper of Story."

"Except there is no other Keeper," he said. "So be unready Keeper, you."

Willow couldn't tell whether he intended to undermine her resolve or force her to a firmer stand. Why should he even care what she decided to do?

She mulled his words as she netted more fish for him and for her journey. Later when her fish had cooled from the embers of his fire and she was wrapping them in the greenest grasses she could find, she found herself hesitating over those she left for him. Not too many, she warned herself. He would only feed them to the otter.

But later when she hoisted her sack, she relented and lowered it again to remove two more fish for the old man. Let him eat them or waste them on the otter. It wasn't for her to allow or forbid.

When she asked him how she could find the straight way back across the heath, he went outside, pointed, and then led her up past the rock shelter. Again he pointed. "Stones. Markers. Lying in turf now, but still pointing. Each points. You follow. From here," he commanded, as if she had already made a false start. "Then straight from one stone to next."

She nodded, refusing to admit puzzlement. She didn't know much more than she had before. But since he didn't sound eager to assist in her departure, she just kept on nodding and saying, "Yes, I see," although she saw nothing at all.

When she took her leave of him, he seemed barely to understand that she and the dog were not simply retreating inside the rock shelter for the night. Maybe he didn't care.

"I might come again," she told him. "When the days get longer. In the greening season," she added. She didn't ask herself how she would manage to get away from the uncles once she had given herself up to them.

During the long night she woke with a start to listen for howling, but there was none. Beside her the dog groaned and yawned. She was up before dawn, ready to hoist her pouch and sack, yet reluctant to leave this shelter. It had become like a home, her own home. The dog fixed her with his expectant gaze. She returned his look, imploring him silently to come with her.

Once again she found that the gentle hills were deceptive. She mistrusted her own sense of direction, and she had no idea how long it should take to reach the first stone. Finally the dog took the lead. He seemed to understand where she was heading. So they walked on with the morning sun behind them, and she hoped that wasn't too wrong.

At midday she stopped to eat, sharing fish with the dog. She regretted having started out without a good long drink at the lake. There was nothing she could do about it now but keep going. Then, late in the day, rain fell. The dog found hollows that collected shallow puddles, and they both drank their fill.

Willow thought of Great Mother coming upon one standing stone after another. Markers, Wrack had said. Markers from so long ago that no one knew what vanished people had raised them. Probably Great Mother had been seeking their story. Whatever she had learned she hadn't shared with Willow, because an unready Keeper must not be burdened with more knowledge than she can store. Bit by bit, Great Mother would say as she gradually offered up stories that were parts of the Story. Willow had to absorb each word, each lilting sound, until she could recite the telling without a single lapse.

"I was almost ready," Willow whispered aloud. Hearing her, the dog came to a halt and turned back to face her. She was tempted then to speak out, to tell him how much she needed him. She resisted that impulse.

On her third day Willow stumbled onto a recumbent stone. Not the first or second, she supposed. She had missed those. But there was no way to be sure which this was and how far she had come. She looked it over for shadow shapes, but there were none. A depression in the turf might be what remained of the hole in which it had stood. She could tell nothing else except where the stone pointed. This way, she told herself. "This way," she said to the dog. He obliged her by lifting his leg against it.

The dog found one more stone. She was so drenched that she nearly passed it. But he stopped so long to sniff and mark it that she backed up to position herself and confirm her direction. Then she slogged on across the heath.

By the time she glimpsed branches ahead, all she wanted was respite from the downpours. There wouldn't be shelter under the bare trees, but at least she would be less exposed to the wind. She was glad she hadn't worn the sheepskin over her head and shoulders. At least now she and the dog would begin their sleep under a dry cover.

There in the valley they huddled, somehow finding comfort if not warmth in closeness.

29

Before they left the valley of trees, the dog feasted on voles while Willow tried to warm herself with half-frozen fish that she pretended came straight off the hearth.

She started the last leg of her journey envying the dog and rethinking her decision to return to her people. After all, she argued with herself as she strode forward, old Wrack was as much her people as were the People of the Singing Seals who lived in dread. When they shunned Great Mother and denied her Story, which was their own, they cast themselves loose from the understanding that connects people with all of life. They were no more rooted now than storm-tossed kelp that washes up on any beach.

Willow wasn't sure why she was returning to people who denied their Story and its Keeper. They would deny her, too, but not because she was unready. They didn't know what they didn't know.

Well, of course they knew that the fathers and mothers of their fathers and mothers were among the few who survived the Wave's devastation. But surely the uncles ought to know that the desperation and reckless greed that followed the Wave had parted the survivors. At the very least the uncles should wonder how resentment and revenge had come to define the barrier that kept them apart. Or were they so gripped by fear that nothing mattered but increasing their number so that the People of the Singing Seals might not die out, their stone huts left to the blowing sands and the treacherous sea?

Now that Willow was thinking of her father and Uncle Redstone, she realized that she had never heard them question how they lived. No wonder they had banished Great Mother. All at once Willow found herself smiling as she strode forward. If the uncles took offense at the story she brought them, maybe they would banish her too.

As she passed the work area where she and the boys and Hazel had crafted the boat, her steps quickened. Soon she would see Crab. This night she might sleep on sealskin in her warm bed closet.

But she wouldn't reach the underground huts before nightfall. So maybe she should plan her approach. It would help to find one of the boys before she showed herself to her father and the uncles or Tall Reed and the other women. But that would scarcely put off what was bound to come next. Once Willow was among them all, she would be forced to submit to their ways.

The dog bounded ahead of her. Before she smelled smoke and heard the wind-driven waves beyond the dunes, the squeals and whimpers of greeting from the dog pack informed her that she had arrived. She slowed and then felt her way toward the cluster of huts.

As soon as she came alongside the shell heap, she could tell exactly where she was. A few more steps to the entrance. She didn't need to see. Stooping until she was inside the passageway, she paused again. Voices reached her. Losing her nerve, she ducked inside the work space where Thorn had stayed and drawn his shadow shapes. And left the fire stone for her to find.

Footsteps came along the passage. Someone was in the work space with her. She shrank back against the wall. "Too dark," muttered the person. Willow recognized that cross tone: Tall Reed. Willow held her breath until the woman stamped down the passageway. "You," she heard Tall Reed command. "Fetch a clay pot, no crack."

There was a shuffling, and then someone else entered the work place. No, there were two of them.

"Is it here?" asked a familiar voice. It was Thistle.

"Left outside," came the reply. Crab.

"Do not speak," Willow said to them. "Not a word."

One of them gasped. It became so still inside the work place that she could hear voices from huts along the passage.

"Will someone come looking for you?" she asked in an undertone.

Crab spoke but didn't answer. "Willow." It was all he said.

"Yes," she replied.

"Everyone thought you must be dead. Where did you go?"

"The forbidden land," she told him. Told Crab. "I would have stayed, but I had dread of being alone." She faltered.

"You were not struck down?" asked Thistle.

"It is a fair land," she assured him. "I have not yet seen the whole of it. I would go back," she said. Wrack's urging released the words she spoke. "I would go back if someone came with me. There is a living there, a kind of living. Different."

"It is forbidden. We will be struck down if we cross into that land."

"I tell you I was not struck down," Willow said. "Great Mother was never struck, and she went often. Here I am now. Unhurt."

"Hazel tried to go after you. She was too weak," Crab said. "She tried. She fell."

"She lived!" exclaimed Willow. "Hazel is alive?"

"Alive and soon to belong to Twin Trunk Tree," Thistle replied. "She was still poorly at the last moonrise. She must grow stronger. The time approaches again. For Twin Trunk Tree," he added bitterly.

"She is willing?" Willow asked.

"She is almost a woman. She accepts. She obeys."

Willow couldn't fathom such obedience. Still, she thought with mounting wonder, Hazel had tried to follow her. "And do you accept also?" she pressed.

Neither boy replied.

It came to Willow that chance was on her side. Here they had come, the companions of all her young days. She had eluded Tall Reed, who might have sent another to fetch a clay pot with no crack. Chance had brought Crab and Thistle, while somewhere nearby, Hazel waited for the moon to begin to swell toward fullness.

"You do not have to live like this," she said to the boys. "It is not the only way. You must know what I learned about our fathers' fathers, the uncles of our uncles. They ravaged the Others." She could almost feel the boys pull back from her. "Listen," she continued. "We were never told that the Others were harmless once, harmless until wronged. What I say is true. If you trust me, if you choose to begin anew, I will explain more, everything. But not now. Now you must make haste. Gather up your precious things, bone tools and sheepskins and seal meat. Gather them quickly and go to the valley. Wait there for me."

"The uncles will not allow us to go," Crab said. "They will stop us."

"We will be leaving Hazel," Thistle objected.

"So bring her," Willow retorted. "If she chooses to come."
Willow doubted that Hazel would abandon certain safety for
the forbidden land of the Others. "And if you choose too, you
must leave before anyone suspects your intentions."

"It is sudden," Thistle said.

"Yes," Willow agreed. "There is no other way."

"It is always sudden with you," Crab told her.

"I know. But I am changed." She smiled a bit. "Somewhat
changed," she added. "We need darkness to put distance
behind us. We need..." She paused, thinking of all the tools
and coverings she could have used in the forbidden land. But
all that came to her now was the comfort she had found in the
sack that Crab had provided. "Berries," she said, sounding
more buoyant than she felt.

She wished she could see their faces. Their eyes would
reveal how likely they were to take her at her word and join
her. They might yet reject the very thought of the abrupt break
she urged. "Packs of berries," she declared, as if they were
planning to meet at the base of the sea stack and she had just
challenged them to a climbing contest.

30

Willow had the wit to ask for the clay pot. She herself would bring it to Tall Reed.   That turned the boys sluggish. They needed to know more before they could believe her. She forced herself to stay calm. Ignoring their questions, she asked them whether they could find their way to the valley of trees in the dark. Of course they could, they retorted. Dark was not the trouble. Trouble was the trouble.

Desperate now, she taunted them. "Maybe I ask too much. Of course you are not quite men. Naturally you unfortunate boys are fearful of following one girl's path, which was Great Mother's path many times over."

Nettled, the boys protested. Reluctance did not grow from fear, they insisted, but from their lifelong obligation to the People of the Singing Seals.

She felt like smacking them, but she held her temper and declared that they had listened without hearing her. She found patience as trying as waiting, but she knew that if she lost her patience now she would lose the boys too.

"Hear me one more time," she said between clenched jaws. She repeated what she had already told them so that they might understand that the Others had once been People of the Singing Seals. She explained again that if they were to begin their lives anew, they must go at once while no one suspected what they intended.

"Tall Reed will come looking for us, because of the clay pot," said Crab. "If we are not here—"

"I told you I will take it to her," Willow responded. She

moved toward the boys, extending her hand. "Let me have it," she said to Crab, realizing that he had shifted from resistance to considering what she proposed. "You have little time," she said as she stepped back to allow them to talk between themselves. "Especially if you wish to stop for Hazel."

Hazel was a danger. Her timidity might snag Thistle, especially if he was not strongly convinced. Yet she possessed a kind of power as well. She was both lure and drag.

"They will never let her go," Thistle said to Crab.

Willow said, "If you make ready now, if Hazel makes ready, you go together before anyone notices. I will bring the clay pot. I can distract them."

Crab wouldn't hand her the pot. He walked out of the work space. A moment later Willow heard Tall Reed's voice raised in indignation, demanding to know what had taken him so long.

"Hazel next," he declared when he rejoined Thistle and Willow.

"Take care," Willow said. "If only one woman or uncle sees you pack your belongings, an alarm can be raised."

"You may be right," Crab admitted. "I was right to deliver the pot, but there is certain advantage in getting away at once."

For a moment they mulled the situation, each of them trying to see how it was likely to play out.

Thistle was the first to speak. "I will go to Hazel while Crab packs for all of us. Hazel may not come, but we ought to plan as though she will."

Willow was startled to hear Thistle, who had always been the least reliable of them, sound so resolute and clear. Maybe the strain of her disappearance and Hazel's near death had changed him too. She hoped so. They needed each other as never before.

She said, "As soon as you leave here, I will show myself to all in my home hut."

"And not come with us?" asked Crab.

"I will have the attention of my father and some uncles and their women. I will make them understand that they are ever barred from the forbidden land." She felt Crab's hand on her arm. "Have no fear," she said to Crab, sensing that he was about to object. "They will not hold me." If she admitted that she was afraid, he might refuse to leave without her. She wanted to tell him that she had transformed herself from promise to threat, but they both knew that the uncles were likely to react as possessively as ever. She would be on her own then. She must manage just one more escape.

31

Waiting near the passage, Willow questioned her reckless plan to confront her father and the uncles. Driven by her dread of isolation, she had made her way home. She would spend this night in the comfort of her own bed closet. At least this one night. And after that? There was no telling when she might be given to an uncle. This much she had risked when first she headed home.

Not now, though. Now she seemed to be about to launch herself over the edge of another cliff. Here she dangled, one leg stabbing at shallow footholds she couldn't see. No telling whether the narrow ledge that seemed to bear the whole of her would keep from crumbling until she could seek the next step down.

If only she could find some sign, a single promise on which to set first one foot and then the other. Where were the boys? Hazel's refusal to join them would have unsettled Thistle. Maybe Crab had to persuade him anew. Willow strained to hear approaching footsteps, but the passage remained empty.

The talk that filtered out from the underground huts blended into a single voice, rising and falling, as lulling as a dream from long ago. Willow recalled listening to that collective voice as she fell asleep. If the boys backed out now, she could still choose that comfort.

Then they came. They were barefoot. She had forgotten to tell them they would need their sealskin boots. She stepped into the passageway, but her warning was stifled as Hazel flung her arms around her. One of the boys, Thistle probably, grabbed Hazel and dragged her after him out into the night.

"Boots," Willow whispered.

"Yes," Crab responded before ducking outside after the other two. "Take care."

Willow drew a deep breath. She listened, this time trying to silence the inside talk so that she might hear the outside scramble over stones and sand and shells. When she was sure that they were on their way, she drew another long breath and walked down to her home hut.

Her father and a few of the uncles were deep in conversation. The women were tending the fire and stuffing seal meat onto stone shelves. Everything looked peaceful. Willow dropped her pouch and pack outside the doorway, then slipped inside. For the longest spell no one took any notice of her. Then the child called Little Gray Bird sidled up to her and proffered the sinew she had been chewing. Willow accepted the gift. She said quietly, "I need seal meat too."

The child nodded and trotted over to the storage shelf to fetch a portion. Only then did Little Gray Bird's mother notice Willow. Only then did she gasp and cry out. The uncles fell silent, first annoyed, then bewildered, and finally astonished.

They rose, the uncles and Willow's father all looming over her as they approached.

She stood her ground, the meat clutched in her hand. Even at this moment when it was vital to show them they couldn't deal with her as they had done before, she held tightly to the meat. She looked for gladness in her father's expression but saw only confusion and alarm. A look the uncles shared.

"We thought you were in the sea," said Uncle Redstone.

Willow's father found his voice: "Where have you been?"

"I walked Great Mother's path," she answered. "To the other side of the valley."

"No one returns from the forbidden land," Uncle Redstone asserted.

"Great Mother did. Often," Willow told him. "You would not hear her. You denied the Story. So I come to tell you what you may not know. So that you may understand."

"Understand?" her father repeated, his voice growing hoarse with anger.

Willow nodded. Her throat tightened. This might be the last time they saw each other. He seemed so far from her still, so remote.

"Did none of you ever hear the story that tells of the People of the Singing Seals raiding the Others and stealing their girls and their young women?"

Out of the bewildered silence, old Uncle Gray Cloud spoke up. "Whispered, yes. There were whispers. Long ago when I was a young boy. I overheard the uncles say the new girls were Others. Then uncles said...told me to cast out what I heard. Long, long ago."

Uncle Redstone nodded. "An old story, and untrue. Our people do not steal. It was the Others who attacked. I know this because my father saw their flung stones. Where they struck, our people were badly maimed, some even killed."

Willow's father said, "We could not allow Great Mother's telling in our Story. It would have festered there, an unseen wound rotting from within. We had to prevent her from spreading that rot. Our fathers and uncles never carried out such a raid."

Willow was beginning to understand. At least Gray Cloud retained a trace of a memory from that time. She said, "Father, you and some of the uncles may be the sons of those girls who were taken. Your mothers' fathers may have been Others."

"It did not happen," Uncle Redstone bellowed. "It never was."

Willow's father only scowled.

Willow said, "I speak for one Other who speaks for all Others who lost children and young women in those raids. He says that after they set aside their grieving, they vowed to stone any who ventured from the valley onto their land. From that time all People of the Singing Seals were forbidden. Only Great Mother was allowed because she was Keeper of Story. And because of her, so was I."

Willow realized that as long as the uncles assumed that Great Mother still lived, they might be able to reconsider what they had stubbornly denied. But Willow had to be careful. They never did favor stories that undercut their self-regard. And if she strayed from the truth, she could walk into a trap of her own making.

Reassure them, she thought. But how? "A day may come when all the People of the Singing Seals will be welcome beyond the valley of trees." She had softened her voice. Now she raised it again. "But only after what was taken is given back. Not until then."

"Those girls grew into women," Uncle Gray Cloud muttered. "They would have grown old by now. They would have died."

"Yes," Willow agreed. "That is why some of us must take their place. I one place, Hazel another."

"Hazel belongs to Twin Trunk Tree," Uncle Redstone thundered.

"Hazel belongs to Hazel," Willow replied evenly.

"She is given," he said.

"She is gone," Willow informed him, terrified that her voice would tremble and betray her. "Already on her way. And before you or anyone else runs after her, consider what lies in wait for you on the forbidden land."

"How many Others are there?" asked Uncle Redstone.

"I cannot say," Willow answered. "If you go after Hazel or me or anyone else from here, you risk finding out. Even the oldest Other can aim and throw with deadly effect. I have seen it." She had overstayed. If Uncle Redstone was coming to his senses, soon her father and the other uncles would too. She needed to be on her way before they matched the story of the Others with the image she had conjured of a mighty force massed beyond the valley.

"Do they demand every one of our few children?" asked her father, grappling with that message. He must still be stunned to see her, to hear her so altered.

"Not at once," Willow said, stalling, wondering how she could end this confrontation. She had to think of a way to withdraw without giving ground. She glanced at the child who had served her seal meat. "Maybe later, when Little Gray Bird and Minnow and Sorrel's baby are able to come on their own, maybe then." Good, she thought. She had mentioned the youngest three, who had not yet been removed from their mothers. That would give Uncle Redstone something more to ponder. Maybe heaping one threat upon another like this would keep him off-balance until she was on her way.

So far she had managed to hold to a kind of truth. But

the going was treacherous; her next assertion could leave her mired in falsehood. Great Mother had always maintained that the Keeper of Story was bound to tell only what she believed to be true. But Willow was too intent on escape to think how to pull back from that mire.

"You said...you said..." Her father stumbled over his words. "Does not Hazel...like each of us...belong to the People of the Singing Seals?"

Here was the way out that Willow sought, a gift from her father. "That is true," she said to him. "But it is also true that before the Wave, we were one people. What changed were the misdeeds of your fathers and their fathers. It was their misdeeds that led to the wrath and revenge that still threaten the People of the Singing Seals."

There, she thought, back on solid ground. Maybe this meant she was ready to be Keeper of Story after all.

32

Outside the huts the black sky glistened, as hard and smooth as the fire stone. Starlight defined the mound of shells and other leavings. Willow felt the usual stab of temptation to look for castoff treasures there.

But this night was different. She must maintain that semblance of calm she had assumed when she turned her back on her father and the uncles. In case one of them might be watching, she had walked with measured step along the darkened passage. As long as she might be seen, it was still necessary to fix her gaze ahead and stride forward.

Stumbling into a sealskin land boat lying directly in her path, she barely managed to keep her balance. Crab must have left it there for her. Well, she would take it then. She shrugged from her shoulders the sack and pouch and placed them on the sealskin bed of the land boat. Seizing the bone grab bar attached at each end to the rawhide drag ropes, she set off.

She was so shaken by the confrontation in the hut that she nearly left without the dog. She paused but didn't dare call out. She needed to be away from this coast and her father and Uncle Redstone. The land boat slid easily over sand and then turf.

The dog appeared, all at once alongside her and matching his easy trot to her vigorous stride. They both needed to eat while they fled. Since she still clutched the seal meat, she tore off a piece with her teeth and handed it down. He took it lightly from between her fingers without touching her hand. Like her, he chewed and swallowed without slowing.

She had never felt so elated and at the same time so exhausted. Without being able to recall everything she had said, she knew she had managed to persuade the uncles and her father to avoid provoking the Others. At least for a while. Of course she had trimmed the truth. How else could she have managed to be here, on her way to join Crab and Thistle and Hazel?

She hadn't planned to resort to hinting at catastrophic outcomes. Those threats had come of their own accord. And they had served their purpose, for they had left her father and the uncles too unsettled to prevent Willow from finishing what she had begun.

Of course she might have left quietly with Crab and Thistle and Hazel. She could be with them now. Sleeping. She ached for sleep almost as intensely as she longed to be with the three of them.

Why then had she stayed behind to confront her father and the uncles? To explain, she reminded herself. Maybe to take proper leave of them, because that was fitting.

These were worthy reasons. Less worthy was the reason that pitted her against all the uncles who had lost their bearings and denied their Story.

So what about her own bearings? When persuasion had failed, when Story went unheard, she had used trickery to prevail against her own people. Never again, though. From now on she would be true to her calling as Keeper of Story.

All these thoughts came at her like fulmars diving from the sky to drive her and the dog from the distant cove they had come to. She found herself running. Only when she had to stop to catch her breath did she realize she could never escape what was embedded within her.

The darkness was beginning to retreat. The dazzling stars dimmed. The three awaiting her were probably still sleeping under sheepskins. Under the naked trees, unlike her on her own first night away. She could scarcely recall why she had recoiled from those trees. It seemed as though another person must have chosen to bed down on the open heath. Long ago and not so long. She glanced down at the dog. He had come to her then. She would never forget that, never forget waking warm, no longer alone.

He halted now, and a low growl rose from his throat. She followed his gaze, astonished to see two upright figures coming toward her.

The dog lowered his head and flicked his good ear forward. When his tail began a slow swing from side to side, she guessed before she could be sure. But why were the boys returning? Why only the two of them?

Willow started forward again. And then she saw that Thistle was dragging a bundled land boat. Hazel? Had she been injured?

Crab and Thistle spoke over each other so that at first Willow couldn't unscramble their jumbled words. Only gradually was she able to hear that they had started back because she had taken so long, because she might be held, because she might have changed her mind, because Hazel was afraid to be so far from home without Willow, because…and because…

"I came as soon as I could," Willow said. "I told you to wait."

"We did wait," Crab responded. "When you did not come, we were unsure."

Thistle said, "It seemed a mistake to leave home for the forbidden land."

Willow shook her head in disbelief. "After all...?" she rasped. "After all I did so the uncles would not interfere?"

Hazel pushed off the coverings and came to stand beside Thistle. "I was cold," she said. "I believed I might never be warm again."

Willow was too drained for anger. She supposed she should have expected that this might happen. She knew these companions. "It is for you to decide," she said to them. "Still," she added, "I will go on. To make a new home."

"Where?" Thistle demanded. "How?"

Willow groped for any argument that might convince him that a real life was possible beyond the valley of trees. But mindful of what she owed them, she was at a loss for words. If there was any hope for a life together, she couldn't skirt the truth. No, nor mislead them, not even Hazel.

"I thought," she began, "I hoped we would take time... find some place we could agree... I have seen but one turf hut and one rock shelter." She dragged the words out of her tiredness, wondering as she heard herself whether she had already spoken them. "There is much turf. For building and for burning. There is rock. There is one last Other, who is old but still can hunt with stones." She rambled slowly. "There is land I have not seen. I did see otter but not the heavy bird that cannot fly. No sheep. Many deer." She was teetering, near to collapse. Standing like this was so much harder than walking.

"You do not have to speak now," Crab told her. "I will go with you."

"Let her continue," Thistle insisted. "I want to hear everything she can tell us."

"I might rest first," Willow mumbled. "Did I tell you Great Mother came? Thorn brought her." Willow wasn't sure she had said that right. What if they expected Great Mother to greet them there? "She sleeps," Willow tried to explain, her words slurred. "Great Mother sleeps. She is safe."

Willow closed her eyes, just for an instant. When she opened them, Hazel was beside her, trying to lead her to the land boat she had just left. Willow staggered over to it and then stood, unable to bend her knees, unable to grasp what was expected of her.

Crab took her by the shoulders, swiveled her, and pushed her down. She would have swatted him, but her delayed impulse slowed every motion to a crawl. Anyway, her arms were useless now that she was lying on her back with a cover descending upon her. She said, "The lake. I forgot to tell…"

33

Willow awoke to agitated voices. It took her a moment to realize she didn't belong to that heated argument. She couldn't see anyone. She didn't want to hear them either. She let herself down into the quiet shallows of sleep and floated away.

She lurched awake when the cover was lifted from her face. Leaning over her, Crab grinned. Fine snow pellets swirled around him, making his face seem to shimmer. She had a feeling she was staring up at his reflection.

"Now it is you who have kept us back," he told her.

Shoving off the sheepskin, she felt the first bite of cold. She squinted because even subdued daylight was painful. "I liked the dark," she murmured.

"It is on its way," he said. "Night."

At this she shot straight up. "I slept through the day?" she exclaimed. "You could have waked me. We need all the day for our journey."

"We have the next day," he told her.

"No," she cried. "We risk...we risk..." But what did they risk here in the valley of trees? Uncle Redstone was unlikely to approach the forbidden land, especially after the scenes of possible reprisal she had conjured up for him to imagine.

Now that she was fully awake, she could smell wood smoke. She peered out beyond the trees. Thistle and Hazel were feeding a flame that sputtered and crackled, tossing sparks into the flying snow. She almost shouted at them to guard against an unwanted fire, but she choked back her warning. Thistle and Hazel were there, still there. Unless she refrained from barking out orders, she would sound like Uncle Redstone or Tall Reed.

Willow rose unsteadily and went to the fire. She said, "If you come now and decide later that it was a mistake, you can always go back. The uncles would welcome you. Twin Trunk Tree would welcome you," she added slyly.

"We know," Hazel told her. "We decided. Again."

Willow couldn't think of a reply. She who might have promised everything could promise nothing. It wouldn't take her companions long to conclude that they had become the new Others.

The dog came and dropped a dead vole in Willow's lap. She set it aside.

Hazel recoiled. "Must we allow such beasts to share our new living space?" she asked.

"You will be glad of him when you hunger for meat and he brings you hare," Willow told her.

Crab, joining them, laughed. "Hazel speaks of this small beast," he told Willow, nudging the vole. "We all accept that the big one goes with you." He dropped two new sealskin boots beside her.

Thistle, half asleep, made an attempt to rouse himself. "Beast?" he asked. Since no one bothered to respond, he leaned back against a rolled sealskin and drowsily suggested that Willow tell them a story to sleep on. "Tell Star the Boundless, the whole of it, all the way to the end," he said.

"The end is unending," Willow responded. "The story of Star the Boundless is in the People's ancient stories. They are in the story of Star just as it is in them. That is how the story lasts. It is remembered."

"Tell," Thistle intoned groggily.

"Food first," Hazel said. "We ate while Willow slept." She rummaged around and brought out a meaty sheep rib, which she handed to Willow.

Yes, food first, Willow agreed as she tore at the meat and sucked the bone and then stripped it thoroughly before licking her hands.

"And this too," said Crab, depositing a portion of dried berries in her cupped palms.

"Oh," she said. "Oh." She tilted back her head and opened her mouth. Here again was a trace of the greening season past and a hint of what was to come. Its flavor was as sharp and intense as before. She licked her blue fingers, but the berry stain remained.

The dog nudged in between Willow and Crab and flopped down deliberately. He nestled close to Willow. Her hand crept over the crumpled ear and rested on the scarred head. Crab's hand reached and for a brief moment covered hers. Then it withdrew.

She glanced through the smoke at Thistle slumped behind the fire. Hazel had drawn a sheepskin over her shoulders, but she was still seated, staring into the flame. Crab was so close to Willow that she felt rather than saw him.

"Story," Thistle prompted.

"Star the Boundless and his companions set out to sea," began Willow, letting the Story unwind. Meanwhile her listening self heard the crackling flame. She spread her arms and leaned forward, warming at this fire that was not of her own making.

Breinigsville, PA USA
10 December 2010
251082BV00002B/6/P